Stories for Girls

by
Hans Christian Andersen

Lovingly Adapted for
Twenty-first Century Children

by
Michael W. Perry
with a Foreword by
George MacDonald

Including Such Well Loved Stories As
The Princess and the Pea
The Little Match Girl
The Little Mermaid
The Ugly Duckling
The Snow Queen
Thumbelina

Inkling Books   Seattle   2001

Editor's Note

All the children's stories in this book were written by Hans Christian Andersen. The editor has modernized the language of old translations from several turn-of-the-century sources, being careful not to alter the original meaning or plot. The goal has been to present these stories as Andersen himself might have written them were he alive today and living in the United States. The graphics have been adapted from illustrations in old collections of these stories. The Foreword entitled "The Imagination" is by George MacDonald, another well-known and much loved writer of children's stories.

Dedication

This book is dedicated to my dear friend Micheii, in the hope that she will find the stories in it as delightful to read as they were for me to edit.

Library Cataloging Data

Andersen, Hans Christian (1805–1875)
Stories for Girls: Lovingly Adapted for Twenty-first Century Children
Editor: Perry, Michael W. [Wiley] (1948–)
147 pages, 7.5 x 9.25 in. 235 x 191 mm.
Includes: 14 chapters and 48 illustrations.
ISBN 1-58742-009-0 (paper)

Inkling Books, Seattle, WA Internet: http://www.InklingBooks.com/
Published in the United States of America on acid-free paper
First Edition, First Printing, June 2001

Contents

Preface 4

Foreword by George MacDonald 5

1. The Princess and the Pea 7

2. Little Ida's Flowers 9

3. Thumbelina 17

4. The Little Mermaid 29

5. The Daisy 49

6. The Wild Swans 53

7. The Ugly Duckling 69

8. The Snow Queen 79

9. The Little Match Girl 111

10. Five Peas in One Pod 115

11. There's No Doubt About It 119

12. The Girl Who Stepped on a Loaf of Bread 122

13. The Jewel of Wisdom 129

14. The Snowdrop 143

Preface

Today, over a century and a quarter after his death, the Danish writer, Hans Christian Andersen, remains one of the world's best-loved writers of children's stories. Generation after generation, something unique about them continues to fascinate children, whatever their cultural background or experiences in life. But with over a hundred English editions of his stories in print, you may ask, "What reason is there for yet another?" The reasons are several.

First, most existing editions are either lengthy collections containing most of his stories or shorter books centering on one or two special ones. There is a need for a more satisfying grouping. For example, some stories have girls as their main character—typically rescuing a brother or friend from trouble. Others center on a boy and his adventures. So, why not a *Stories for Girls* and a *Stories for Boys?* Some may complain, but Andersen himself poked fun at such pretentiousness in "Two Maidens." There he described an official policy to change the name of a tool used by the street pavers of his day from "maiden" to "hand-rammer." Given life and personality by Andersen, the "maidens" themselves complain about the change. The same is true of children. Boys and girls see themselves as different. Why engage in a futile attempt to pound them into a muddle? It makes more sense to give them stories that teach, ever so gently, what it means to be a good girl or a good boy.

Second, a new grouping offers the opportunity to better display Andersen's genius. What could be better for a parent trying to cheer a child than a reliable collection of *Stories that Are Funny?* The same is true for more serious matters. Few writers have been as disturbed by death as Andersen and that concern surfaces in many of his stories. For almost two years I worked on the cancer ward of a children's hospital. I know from experience that there's nothing parents, however loving, can do to keep their child from being exposed to death, even if just of a pet. The question isn't whether they will face death, but how they will learn to face it. Andersen provides answers in *Stories about Dying*.

Finally, there's the issue of modern 'adaptations.' As you will see in this book, Andersen's little mermaid is a far deeper and more complex character than the tale as told by Hollywood. She doesn't seek a kiss, something any pretty girl can easily get. She seeks the exclusive and faithful love of the prince, as well as something far more important, eternal life. The tragedy when she misses the first is redeemed when she finds that she has, without knowing it, won the second. Throughout this book and the others in the series as they are published, I've sought to modernize the language of Andersen's earlier translations for the sake of today's children without altering in the slightest his deep, underlying message. My goal has been to tell these stories exactly as Andersen would have told them were he alive today. The reader may judge whether I have been successful.—Michael W. Perry

.

Foreword

"The Imagination" by George MacDonald

Like Hans Christian Andersen, MacDonald is a much-loved writer of children's stories. In this extract from a 1867 article (republished in his 1893 *A Dish of Oats*), MacDonald answered critics who claimed that fairy tales distract children (particularly girls) from what is practical and useful. Andersen offered similar arguments in "Little Ida's Flowers" with his portrayal of a "dull and sour-faced" critic of "such nonsense" and in "The Snow Queen," when a boy who is being kidnapped tries desperately to pray "but all he could remember was the multiplication table." Children, both wisely tell us, need to exercise their growing imaginations just like they exercise their muscles.

We return now to the class [of people] which, from the first, we supposed hostile to the imagination and its functions generally. Those belonging to it will now say:

> It was to no imagination such as you have been setting forth that we were opposed, but to those wild fancies and vague reveries in which young people indulge, to the damage and loss of the real in the world around them.

"And," we insist, "you would rectify the matter by smothering the young monster at once—because he has wings, and, young to their use, flutters them about in a way discomposing to your nerves, and destructive to those notions of propriety of which this creature—you stop not to inquire whether angel or pterodactyle—has not yet learned even the existence. Or, if it is only the creature's vagaries of which you disapprove, why speak of them as the exercise of the imagination? As well speak of religion as the mother of cruelty because religion has given more occasion of cruelty, as of all dishonesty and devilry, than any other object of human interest. Are we not to worship, because our forefathers burned and stabbed for religion? It is more religion we want. It is more imagination we need. Be assured that these are but the first vital motions of that whose results, at least in the region of science, you are more than willing to accept." That evil may spring from the imagination, as from everything except the perfect love of God, cannot be denied. But infinitely worse evils would be the result of its absence. Selfishness, avarice, sensuality, cruelty, would flourish tenfold; and the power of Satan would be well established ere some children had begun to choose. Those who would quell the apparently lawless tossing of the spirit, called the youthful imagination, would suppress all that is to grow out of it. They fear the enthusiasm they never felt; and instead of cherishing this divine thing, instead of giving it room and air for healthful growth, they would crush and confine it—with but one result of their victorious endeavours—imposthume [abscess], fever, and corruption. And the disastrous consequences would soon appear in the intellect likewise which they worship. Kill that whence spring the crude fancies and wild day-dreams of the young, and you will never lead them beyond dull facts—dull because their relations to each other, and the one life that works in them all, must remain undiscovered. Whoever would have his children avoid this arid region will do well to allow no teacher to approach them—not even of mathematics—who has no imagination.

But although good results may appear in a few from the indulgence of the imagination, how will it be with the many?

We answer that the antidote to indulgence is development, not restraint, and that such is the duty of the wise servant of Him who made the imagination.

But will most girls, for instance, rise to those useful uses of the imagination? Are they not more likely to exercise it in building castles in the air to the neglect of houses on the earth? And as the world affords such poor scope for the ideal, will not this habit breed vain desires and vain regrets? Is it not better, therefore, to keep to that which is known, and leave the rest?

"Is the world so poor?" we ask in return. The less reason, then, to be satisfied with it; the more reason to rise above it, into the region of the true, of the eternal, of things as God thinks them. This outward world is but a passing vision of the persistent true. We shall not live in it always. We are dwellers in a divine universe where no desires are in vain, if only they be large enough. Not even in this world do all disappointments breed only vain regrets. And as to keeping to that which is known and leaving the rest—how many affairs of this world are so well-defined, so capable of being clearly understood, as not to leave large spaces of uncertainty, whose very correlate faculty is the imagination? Indeed it must, in most things, work after some fashion, filling the gaps after some possible plan, before action can even begin. In very truth, a wise imagination, which is the presence of the spirit of God, is the best guide that man or woman can have; for it is not the things we see the most clearly that influence us the most powerfully; undefined, yet vivid visions of something beyond, something which eye has not seen nor ear heard, have far more influence than any logical sequences whereby the same things may be demonstrated to the intellect. It is the nature of the thing, not the clearness of its outline, that determines its operation. We live by faith, and not by sight. Put the question to our mathematicians—only be sure the question reaches them—whether they would part with the well-defined perfection of their diagrams, or the dim, strange, possibly half-obliterated characters woven in the web of their being; their science, in short, or their poetry; their certainties, or their hopes; their consciousness of knowledge, or their vague sense of that which cannot be known absolutely: will they hold by their craft or by their inspirations, by their intellects or their imaginations? If they say the former in each alternative, I shall yet doubt whether the objects of the choice are actually before them, and with equal presentation.

—§§§—

1. The Princess and the Pea

A prince searches in vain for a real princess to be his bride
until one comes to him on a dark and stormy night.
Reading time: 5 minutes. All ages.

Once on a time there was a prince who wanted to marry a princess more than anything else in the whole world. But he did not like phony princesses. No, he insisted that the one he married must be a real one.

So he traveled all over the world trying to find just such a princess. He looked in big countries. He looked in middle-sized countries. He even looked in countries so small you could walk across them in just a few minutes. But nowhere did he find a *real* princess—not a single one. True, there were princesses enough and to spare. The world seemed full of them. Everywhere you turned, you bumped into one. But he had trouble believing they were real ones. There was always something about them that was not as it should be. So he came home from his trip very sad. He began to wonder if there was a real princess left for him to marry.

Then one evening a terrible storm struck his royal city. There was thunder and lightning like you've never seen before. It was incredible! The rain poured down like a flooding river. The thunder boomed like a hundred cannons going off at once. Scariest of all, lightning lit up the sky like a million birthday candles. Just then a knocking was heard at the palace gate. The king—who was of course the prince's father—went to see who would be out on such a dreadful night.

Would you believe there was a princess standing at the gate? But, goodness gracious, with all that wind and rain, she certainly did not *look* like a princess. The water ran in streams from her hair and down her soggy and rumpled clothes. It even ran in the toes of her shoes and out again at the heels, so she went "squish, squish" as she walked. She looked like a poor beggar without a penny in her purse. Yet she solemnly promised the king and queen that she was a real princess.

"Well, we'll soon find that out," thought the old queen. Saying nothing, she went into the guest bedroom. She took all the bedding off the bed frame. Then she put a tiny pea at the bottom. That's all, just one little pea. On top it she put twenty soft mattresses. But that wasn't enough. No, not at all. For good measure, she put twenty downy feather beds on top of the mattresses. Then she went and told the king and prince what she had done. They both smiled.

That was the bed on which the princess had to lie all night. In the morning the queen asked her how she had slept. As the queen did so, she looked slyly at the king and prince.

"Oh, very badly!" said the princess in a very exasperated voice. "I scarcely closed my eyes all night. Heaven only knows what was in that bed, but I was lying on something terribly hard. I am black and blue all over. It was horrible!"

Now they knew beyond a shadow of a doubt that she was a real princess. Why? Because she had felt that one tiny pea through the twenty soft mattresses and twenty downy feather beds. Only a real princess would be as sensitive as that.

The prince was delighted and soon asked her to be his wife. For he knew that at last he had found a real princess. What's more, the pea was put in a museum, where it may still be seen to this day, if no one has stolen it.

There, that is a true story. Or so I have been told.

—§§§—

2. Little Ida's Flowers

From a student, young Ida discovers a delightful and imaginative reason why flowers droop and fade.
Reading time: 25 minutes, 2 parts. Younger children.

"My poor flowers are dead," said little Ida sadly. "They were so pretty yesterday. Now the leaves are hanging down all dry and withered. Why do they do that," she asked the student who sat on the sofa. She liked him very much. He could tell the funniest stories and could cut the prettiest pictures out of paper—pictures of hearts and ladies dancing, of castles with doors that opened, as well as flowers.

"Why do the flowers look so faded today?" she asked again, and pointed to a little nosegay, which was quite withered.

"Don't you know what's the matter with them?" answered the student. "The flowers were at an elegant ball last night, so it is no wonder they hang their heads. They are tired from all that dancing."

"But flowers cannot dance?" cried little Ida.

"Oh yes they can," replied the student. "When it grows dark, and everybody is asleep, they run about quite merrily. They have an elegant ball almost every night."

"Can children go to these balls?"

"Yes," said the student, "little daisies and lilies of the valley."

"Where do the beautiful flowers dance?" asked little Ida.

"Have you seen the large castle outside the town gate where the king lives in summer," answered the student, "the one with beautiful garden full of flowers? Haven't you fed the swans who live there bread when they swam up to you? Well, believe me, the flowers have wonderful balls in that very castle."

"I was in the castle garden yesterday with my mother," said Ida. "But all the leaves were off the trees, and there was not a single flower left. Where are they? I used to see so many in the summer."

"They are all in the castle," replied the student. As soon as the king and all the court go into the town for the winter, the flowers run out of the garden and into the castle. You should see how happy they are inside. The two most beautiful roses seat themselves on the king's throne and become the king and queen. Then all the red cockscombs range themselves on each side and bow. These are the lords-in-waiting. After that the pretty flowers come in, and there is a grand ball. The blue violets represent young naval cadets and dance with hyacinths and crocuses, which they call young ladies. The tulips and tiger lilies are the old ladies who sit and watch the dancing, to make sure everything is done properly and in order."

"But," said little Ida, "is there no one there to punish the flowers for dancing in the king's castle without his permission?"

"No one knows about it," said the student. "The old steward of the castle, who watches there at night, sometimes comes in. But he carries a big bunch of keys. As soon as the flowers hear the keys rattle, they hide behind the long curtains and stand very still, just peeping their heads out. Then the old steward says, 'I smell flowers here,' but he cannot see them."

"Oh, how wonderful," said little Ida, clapping her hands. "Would I be able to see these flowers?"

"Yes," said the student, "be sure and remember what I have told you the next time you go out. If you peep through a castle window, I'm sure you will see them. I did today, and I saw a long yellow lily lying stretched out on a sofa. She was a court lady."

"Can the flowers from the Botanical Gardens go to these balls?" asked Ida. "It's such a long way!"

"Oh yes," said the student "whenever they like, for they can fly. Haven't you seen those beautiful red, white and yellow butterflies that look like flowers? They *were* flowers once. They fly off their stalks into the air and flap their petals as if they were little wings. If they behave well, they get permission to fly about during the day, instead of having to sit on their stems. In time their petals become real wings, and they become real butterflies.

"Actually, I'm not sure about one thing. The flowers in the Botanical Gardens may have never been to the king's palace. If so, they know nothing about the dancing that takes place there each night. I'll tell you what you can do to surprise the professor who lives down the street. You know him don't you, the one who studies plants and writes long books about them? Well, next time you go into his garden, tell one of the flowers that there will be a grand ball at the castle that evening. Then that flower will tell all the others, and they will fly away to the castle that very night. The next time professor walks into his garden, there will not be a single flower left. Then he will wonder what happened to them, and that will be funny!"

"But how can one flower tell another? Flowers can't talk!"

"Certainly not," replied the student. "But they can make signs. Haven't you seen how, when the wind blows, they nod at each another and rustle their green leaves? That's how they talk to each other."

"Does the professor understand their signs?" asked Ida.

"Yes, I am sure he does. He went one morning into his garden and saw a stinging nettle making signs with its leaves to a beautiful red carnation. It was saying, 'You are so pretty, I like you very much.' But the professor did not approve of such nonsense. So he clapped his hands on the nettle to stop it. Then the leaves, which are its fingers, stung him so sharply that he has never tried to touch a nettle since."

"Oh how funny!" said Ida, and she laughed.

"How can anyone put such *nonsense* in a child's head?" said a dull and sour-faced lawyer, who had come for a visit and now sat on the sofa. He disliked the student and would grumble when he saw the boy cutting out his odd and amusing pictures. Sometimes it would be a man hanging from a rope and holding a heart in his hand, as if he had been stealing hearts. Sometimes it was an old witch riding through the air on a broom and carrying her husband on her nose. But this lawyer did not like jokes and would always say, "How can anyone put such nonsense in a child's head? What crazy tales they are!"

But to little Ida, all the stories the student told her were funny, and she thought about them a lot. The flowers did hang their heads because they had been dancing all night. They were very tired, and some might even be sick. So she took them to her playroom, where some toys lay on a little table and the drawer was filled with toys.

Sophy, her doll, lay in a doll's bed asleep. So little Ida said to her, "You must get up Sophy and lie in the drawer tonight. For the poor flowers are ill and must lie in your bed, so they can get well."

Then she took out the doll, who looked quite cross and said not a single word, for she was angry at being put out of her bed. Ida placed the flowers in the doll's bed and drew a quilt over them. She told them to lie very still and be good. She would make some tea for them, so they could get well and get up the next morning. Then she drew the curtains around the little bed, so the sun would not shine in their eyes.

During the whole evening, she thought about what the student had told her. Before she went to bed, she could not resist. She just had to peep through the curtains into the garden where all her mother's beautiful flowers grew, hyacinths, tulips, and many others. She whispered to them quite softly, "I know you are going to a ball tonight."

But the flowers looked as if they did not understand, and not a leaf moved. Still Ida felt quite sure they knew all about it. She lay awake for a long time after she went to bed, thinking about how pretty it would be to see all the beautiful flowers dancing in the king's garden. "I wonder if my flowers have really been there," she said to herself, and then she fell asleep.

Ida Awakens

In the middle of the night Ida woke up. She had been dreaming of flowers and the student, as well as the boring lawyer who found fault with him. It was very quiet in her bedroom. The night light burned on the table, and her father and mother were asleep.

"I wonder if my flowers are still lying in Sophy's bed," she thought to herself. "I would like to know very much." So she raised herself up and looked at the door of the playroom where all her flowers and toys lay. It was partly open. As she listened, it seemed as if someone in the room was playing the piano, but softly and more prettily than she had ever heard before.

"All the flowers must be dancing in there," she thought. "Oh how much I would like to see them." But she did not dare move for fear of waking up her father and mother. "If the flowers would only come in here," she thought. But they did not come, and the music continued to play so beautifully that she could resist no longer. She crept out of her little bed, went softly to the door, and looked into the room. Oh, what a wonderful sight she saw!

There was no night light burning, but the room was bright, for the moon was shining through the window on to the floor, and that made it almost like day. All the hyacinths and tulips stood in two long rows down the room. Not a single flower remained in the window, and the flowerpots were all empty. The flowers were dancing gracefully on the floor, making dance turns and holding each other by their long green leaves as they swung gracefully around.

At the piano sat a large yellow lily that little Ida was certain she had seen that summer. She remembered the student saying that this flower looked very much like Miss Lina, one of Ida's friends. They all laughed at him then. But now it seemed to little Ida as if the tall, yellow flower really was like that young lady. She acted the same way while playing, bending her long yellow face from side to side, and nodding in time to the beautiful music.

Then Ida saw a large purple crocus jump on to the middle of the table where the toys stood, go up to the doll's bedstead, and draw back the curtains. There lay the sick flowers, but they quickly got up and nodded to the others as a sign that they wanted to dance. An old tattered doll with a broken mouth stood up and bowed to the pretty flowers. The flowers did not look sick now, but jumped about and were merry. They were so busy, no one noticed little Ida watching.

Then something fell from the table. Ida looked and saw that a wooden rod with three legs had jumped down among the flowers, as if it belonged with them. Sitting on it was little wax doll with a broad brimmed hat much like the one worn by the lawyer. The wooden rod hopped about among the flowers on its three feet and stamped loudly, as it danced a Polish folk dance. The flowers could not do that. They were much too light to make noise when they stamped their feet.

Then the wax doll who was riding on the wooden rod seemed to grow larger and taller. He turned and said to the paper dolls, "How can you put such silly things in a child's head? They are all foolish fancies." Then the wax doll became exactly like the lawyer with his broad brimmed hat. He even looked dull and sour. But the paper dolls struck him on his thin legs, and he shrank up again and became nothing but a little wax doll. That was very amusing, and Ida could not keep from laughing.

The wooden rod went on dancing, and the lawyer was forced to dance along. It was no use. He might make himself great and tall or remain a little wax doll with a large black hat, still he must dance, like it or not. At last the flowers helped him, especially those who had been resting in the doll's bed. They got the wooden rod to quit dancing.

At the same time a loud knocking was heard in the drawer where Ida's doll, Sophy, lay with many other toys. A doll like a chimney sweep ran to the end of the table, lay down, and pulled the drawer out.

Sophy raised himself up and looked around quite astonished, "There must be a ball here tonight," she said. "Why didn't somebody tell me?"

"Will you dance with me?" said the chimney sweep, all covered with black ashes.

"You are the right sort to dance with, certainly," she said cruelly, turning her back on him.

Sophy sat on the edge of the drawer, hoping one of the flowers would ask her to dance. But no one came up to her. So she coughed, "Hem, hem, a-hem," to get attention. But still no one came.

The shabby chimney sweep was dancing alone and not badly either. Since none of the flowers seemed to notice Sophy, she let herself down from the drawer to the floor, making a loud noise. All the flowers came up to her and asked if she had hurt herself, especially those who had been resting in her bed. But she was not hurt at all. Ida's flowers then thanked her for the use of her nice bed and were kind to her. They led her into the middle of the room, where the moon shone, and danced with her, while all the other flowers formed a circle around them. Sophy was happy with all this attention and said they might keep her bed. She did not mind lying in the drawer at all.

The sick flowers thanked her very much and said, "We cannot live much longer. Tomorrow morning we will be dead. Please tell little Ida to bury us in the garden near the canary's grave. Then in the summer we will wake up and be more beautiful than ever."

"No, you must not die," said Sophy sadly, as she kissed the flowers.

At that moment, the door of the room opened, and a number of beautiful flowers danced in. Ida could not imagine where they came from, unless they were flowers from the king's garden. First came two lovely roses, with golden crowns on their heads. These were the king and queen. Beautiful stocks and carnations followed, bowing to everyone who was there. They had brought music with them. Large poppies and peonies had pea shells for instruments and blew into them until they were red in the face. The bunches of blue hyacinths and the little white snowdrops jingled their flowers as if they were real bells. Then came many more flowers—blue violets, purple heart's-ease, daisies, and lilies of the valley. They all danced together and kissed each other. It was *very* beautiful.

At last the flowers wished each other good night. Then little Ida slipped back into her bed and dreamed about all she had seen. When she woke up the next morning, she went quickly to the little table to see if the flowers were still there. She drew aside the curtains of the doll bed. There they all lay, but quite faded, much more so than the day before. Sophy was lying in the drawer where Ida had placed her, but she looked very sleepy.

"Do you remember what the flowers told you to say to me?" said little Ida. But Sophy looked quite stupid and said nothing.

"You are not kind at all," said Ida, "and yet they all danced with you."

Then she took a little paper box, on which were painted beautiful birds, and put the dead flowers in it.

"This shall be your pretty coffin," she said. "By and by, when my cousins come to visit, they will help me bury you in the garden, so next summer you can grow up more beautiful than ever."

Her cousins were two good boys named James and Adolphus. Their father had given each of them a bow and arrow, which they brought to show Ida. She told them about the poor flowers that had died. As soon as they got permission from her parents, they went out with her to bury the flowers.

The two boys walked first, with bows on their shoulders. Little Ida followed, carrying the pretty box with the dead flowers. They dug a little grave in the garden. Ida kissed her flowers and laid them and the box in the ground. James and Adolphus then fired their bows over the grave, for they had neither guns nor cannons.

That, my friend, is the story of Little Ida and her flowers.

—§§§—

3. Thumbelina

A very tiny girl travels the world, meeting all sorts of
interesting people and creatures, good and bad.
Reading time: 40 minutes, 2 parts. All ages.

There was once a woman who wished very much to have a little child. Unfortunately, she did not have any idea where she could get one. Years passed and her wish never, ever came true. At last she went to a fairy and asked, "I would like so much to have a little child. Can you tell me where I might find one?"

"Oh, that is easily done," said the fairy with a smile. "Here is a seed that is very different from those that grow in farmer's fields or that chickens eat. Put it in a flowerpot and see what happens."

"Thank you," said the woman, and she gave the fairy twelve dollars, which is a lot to pay for one small seed. Then she went home and planted it. Soon, a large, beautiful flower grew and bloomed. It looked like a tulip, but its petals stayed closed like the bud of a rose.

"It's such pretty flower," said the woman, as she kissed the red and gold leaves. When she did that, the flower opened, and she saw that it was a real tulip. But that was *not* the most amazing thing about it. Inside the flower was a very delicate and graceful little girl. She was only half as long as a thumb, so the woman gave her the name "Thumbelina."

A walnut shell, elegantly polished, became the baby cradle and her bedsheets were made of soft and silky flower petals. During the day little Thumbelina played on a table, where the woman had placed a bowl full of water. Around the bowl were flowers with their stems stuck in the water. On the water floated a tulip leaf, which Thumbelina had turned into a boat. Here the little girl sat and rowed from one side of the bowl to the other, with two oars made of white horsehair. If you had seen it, you would have agreed. It was very pretty sight.

Thumbelina also had a beautiful voice. She could sing so softly and sweetly that no one had ever heard such beautiful music before

One night, as she lay in her walnut-shell bed, an slimy mother toad hopped through a broken pane of glass in the window of Thumbelina's room and jumped on the table where she lay sleeping beneath her rose petal sheets. "What a pretty wife this little girl would make for my son," said the mother toad. So she put the walnut shell in which Thumbelina lay asleep in her mouth and then jumped through the window and out into the garden.

Now the mother toad lived with her son on the marshy side of a stream that ran through the garden. And, if you can believe it, the son was even *uglier* than his mother. He also wasn't much for conversation. When he saw the pretty little girl sleeping in her elegant bed, all he could say was, "Croak, croak, croak."

"Don't speak so loud, or she will wake up," said the mother toad. "Then she might run away, for she is as light as swan's feather. We will place her on one of the water lily pads in the stream. It will be like an island to her, she is so small and light. Then she cannot escape. While she is a prisoner there, we will fix up a room under the marsh where the two of you can live after you are married."

Far out in the stream there were water lilies with broad green pads that floated on top of the water. The old mother toad swam to largest of them with the walnut shell in which little Thumbelina lay sound asleep. Early the next morning, the little girl woke up and began to cry bitterly when she discovered where she was. She had good reason to be sad, for she could see nothing but water all around her with no way to reach land and escape.

Meanwhile, the old mother toad was busy under the marsh, decorating her son's new room with rushes and wild yellow flowers to make it look pretty for her new daughter-in-law. Then she swam out with her ugly son to the leaf on which she had placed poor little Thumbelina. She wanted to fetch the bed, so she might put it in the bridal chamber for little Thumbelina. The mother toad bowed to the little girl and said, "Here is my son, he will be your husband. You will live happily in the marsh by the stream."

"Croak, croak, croak," was all her son could say. The mother toad took up the elegant little bed and swam away with it, leaving Thumbelina all alone on the green leaf, where she sat down and wept. She could not bear to think of living with the old mother toad and having her dull son as a husband. The little fishes, who swam about in the water beneath, had seen the two toads and heard what was said. They lifted their heads out of the water to look at the little maiden. As soon as they caught sight of her, they saw she was very pretty. It made them very sad to think that she must go and live with the ugly toads.

"No, this must never be!" they cried. So they got together underwater around the green stalk that held the water lily pad on which the little girl sat crying. Working quickly, they gnawed it away with their teeth. Then the lily pad floated down the stream, carrying Thumbelina far away.

Thumbelina floated past many towns. The little birds in the bushes saw her and sang, "What a lovely little creature." The lily pad drifted farther and farther, until it carried her to another country. A graceful white butterfly constantly fluttered around her, as if he wanted to meet her. At last he got up his courage and landed on the lily pad. Meeting Thumbelina made the butterfly very happy, and she was happy to see him too. She was now so far away that the mean mother toad would never find her.

The country through which Thumbelina was floating was more beautiful than you could ever imagine. The sun shone on the water until it glittered like gold. She took off her the tiny ribbon that was her belt and tied one end of it around her friend, the butterfly. The other end she fastened to the lily pad. With the butterfly's help, it now glided along much faster than ever, taking her far away from the toads.

But that happiness was not to last. Soon a large beetle flew by. The moment he caught sight of her, he seized her around her delicate waist with his claws and flew off with her to a tree. The lily pad continued down the brook, and the butterfly with it, for he was fastened to it and could not get away to help her.

How frightened little Thumbelina felt when the beetle flew her to the tree! She was especially sorry for the beautiful white butterfly she had tied to the lily pad. For if he could not free himself, he would die of hunger. But the beetle was selfish and did not care about that. He sat by her side on a large green leaf and gave her some honey from the flowers to eat. He told her she was very pretty, though she did not look the least like a beetle. Soon, however, all the other beetles came by, turned up their feelers and said, "She has only two legs! How ugly that looks." "She has no feelers," said another. "Her waist is quite slim. Pooh! In fact, she looks just like a human being only smaller. Ugh!"

"Oh! She is ugly," said all the lady beetles, although Thumbelina was very pretty. Then the beetle who had stolen her believed all the others when they said she was ugly. He would have nothing more to do with her and told her she could go where she liked. Then he flew down with her from the tree and placed her on a daisy. She wept at the thought that she was so ugly that even the beetles would have nothing to do with her. All the while she was really the loveliest creature that you could imagine, as soft and delicate as a beautiful rose leaf.

During that whole summer, poor little Thumbelina lived all alone in the forest. She was very clever. She wove a bed with blades of grass and hung it under a leaf that protected her from the rain. She sucked the honey from the flowers for food and drank the dew from their leaves every morning. That is how she spent the summer and autumn. Except for being all alone, it was wonderful.

But then came the winter—a long, cold winter. The birds who had sang to her so sweetly flew away. The trees and the flowers that were so pretty dropped their leaves or withered away. The large clover leaf under which she lived, rolled up and shrivelled until nothing remained but a yellow stalk. Worst of all, Thumbelina felt *dreadfully* cold, for her clothes were torn. She was so frail and delicate that she almost froze to death. It began to snow too. Because she was so tiny, the snowflakes falling on her were like a whole shovelful of snow being dumped on you or I. For we are tall, but she was only an inch high.

Trying to keep warm, Thumbelina wrapped herself up in a dry leaf. But it cracked in the middle and did not keep out the cold, so she shivered terribly. Near the forest in which she had been living lay a cornfield, but its corn had been cut a long time ago. Nothing remained but dry stubble standing in frozen ground. To her, trying to cross that field to find shelter was like one of us struggling through a large forest overgrown with bushes. How she shivered from the cold as she stumbled along! It was very sad.

At last, she came to the door of a field mouse, who had a little den under the corn stubble. There the field mouse lived in warmth and comfort with a whole roomful of corn to eat, a kitchen, and a beautiful dining room. Poor little Thumbelina stood in front of the door, just like a little beggar girl, and begged for a small seed, for she had been without anything to eat for two whole days.

"You poor little creature," said the field mouse, who was a kind person. "Come into my warm room and dine with me." She was very pleased with Thumbelina, so she said, "You are welcome to stay with me all winter if you like. But you must keep my rooms clean and neat. You must also tell me stories, for I like to hear them very much." Thumbelina did all the field mouse asked and found herself very comfortable.

A Mole Visits the Field Mouse

"We will have a visitor soon," said the field mouse one day. "My neighbor comes to see me once a week. He is better off than I am. He has large rooms in his house and wears a beautiful black velvet coat. If you had him for a husband, you would be well provided for. But he is blind, so you must tell him some of your prettiest stories."

But Thumbelina did not feel at all interested in this neighbor, for he was a mole and lived under the cold, damp ground. However, he came dressed in his black velvet coat.

"He is very rich and educated, and his house is twenty times larger than mine," said the field mouse. Such things impressed her.

He was rich and educated, no doubt, but he always spoke badly of the sun and pretty flowers, because he had never seen them. Thumbelina was forced to sing to him, "Ladybird, ladybird, fly away home," and many other songs. As a result, the mole fell in love with her because she had such a sweet voice. But he said nothing yet, for he was very cautious.

A short time before, the mole had dug a long passage under the ground from his own home to that of the field mouse. The field mouse had permission to walk with Thumbelina in the passage whenever she liked. But he warned them not to be alarmed at the sight of a dead bird that lay in the passage. It was a beautiful bird and could not have been dead long.

The mole took a piece of glowing wood in his mouth, and it glittered like cold fire in the dark. He went before them to light the way through the long, dark passage.

When they came to the spot where the dead bird lay, the mole pushed his nose through the ceiling and the ground gave way. There was now a large hole above, and daylight shone into the passage. In the middle of the floor lay swallow, as still as death, his beautiful wings pulled close to his sides, his feet and his head drawn up under his feathers. The poor bird must have died from the cold, Thumbelina thought. It made little her very sad to see that, for she loved little birds. All summer they had sang and twittered for her so beautifully.

But the mole pushed the bird aside with his crooked legs and said, "He will sing no more now. How miserable it must be to be born a little bird. I'm glad none of *my* children will ever be birds. For birds do nothing but sing, 'Tweet, tweet' and always die of hunger in the winter."

"Yes, you may well say that, as a clever mole," said the field mouse. "What is the use of this bird's twittering, for when winter comes he must either starve or freeze to death. Still birds are a very high bred."

Thumbelina said nothing. But when the other two had turned their backs on the bird, she stooped down, pushed aside the soft feathers that covered the bird's head, and kissed the closed eyelids. "Perhaps this was one who sang to me so sweetly in the summer," she said. "How much pleasure you gave me, you dear, pretty bird."

The mole then plugged up the hole through which the daylight shone and took the two ladies home. But during the night Thumbelina could not sleep. She got out of bed and wove a large, beautiful carpet of hay and carried it to the dead bird. She spread it over him and added some light, feathery down from flowers she found in the field mouse's home. It was as soft as wool, and she spread some of it on each side of the bird, so he might lie warmly on the cold ground. "Farewell, pretty bird," said she. "Farewell and thank you for your delightful singing during the summer, when all the trees were green, and the warm sun shone on us."

Then she put her head on the bird's breast and became frightened. For it seemed as if something inside the bird went "thump, thump." It was the bird's heart. He was not really dead, only numbed from the cold. The warm blanket was bringing him back to life. In autumn, all swallows fly away to warm countries. But if one happens to linger a little too long, the cold seizes it and it becomes frozen, falling down as if dead. It remains where it fell, and the cold snow covers it.

Thumbelina trembled. She was frightened, for the bird was large, much larger than she was. After all, she was only an inch high. But she took courage and laid the wool more thickly over the poor swallow. Then she took the leaf that she used for her own blanket, and laid it over the poor bird's head.

The next morning she slipped out of the field mouse's house to see the bird. He was alive but very weak. He could only open his eyes for a moment to look at Thumbelina, who stood by holding a piece of glowing decayed wood in her hand, for she had no other lantern. "Thank you, pretty little maiden," said the sick swallow. "I have been so nicely warmed by you, that I will soon regain my strength and fly about again in the warm sunshine."

"Oh," said she, "it is cold out of doors now. It snows and freezes. Stay in your warm bed. I will take care of you until the spring." She brought the swallow some water in a flower petal. After he drank, he told her that he had hurt one of his wings on a thornbush and could not fly as fast as the others, who were soon far away in their journey to warm countries.

At last, too tired to go on, he had fallen to the ground and could remember no more, not even how he came to be under the ground, where she had found him. That whole winter the swallow remained underground, and Thumbelina nursed him with kindness and love. Neither the mole nor the field mouse knew anything about it, for they did not like swallows.

Soon spring came, and the sun warmed the ground. As Thumbelina opened the hole in the ceiling that the mole had made, the swallow said farewell to her. The sun shone in on them so beautifully that the swallow asked her if she would go with him. She could sit on his back, he said, and he would fly away with her into the green forest. But Thumbelina knew it would make the field mouse sad if she left that way, so she said, "No, I cannot."

"Farewell, then, farewell, you good, pretty little maiden," said the swallow. Then he flew out of the tunnel and into the sunshine.

Thumbelina looked after him, and tears came to her eyes. She was very fond of the poor swallow.

"Tweet, tweet," sang the bird, as he flew into the green forest and out of sight. Thumbelina felt very sad. She could not go into the warm sunshine. Corn had been planted in the field over the house of the field mouse. It had grown so high, that it created what looked like a thick forest to Thumbelina, who—you may remember—was only an inch high.

"You are going to be married, Thumbelina," said the field mouse one day. "My neighbor has asked for you. What good fortune for a poor child like you. Now we will prepare your wedding clothes. They must be of wool and linen. Nothing should be lacking when you become the mole's wife."

Though she hated it, Thumbelina had to turn the spindle, and the field mouse hired four spiders, who were to weave day and night. Every evening the mole visited her and kept speaking of the time when the summer would be over. Then he would marry little Thumbelina. But for now the heat of the sun was so great that it burned the ground and made it as hard as stone. As soon as the summer was over, he said, the wedding would take place.

But Thumbelina was not at all pleased, for she did not like the dull mole. Every morning when the sun rose, and every evening when it went down, she would slip out the door of the mouse's home. As the wind blew the ears of corn about, she could catch a glimpse of the blue sky. She thought of how beautiful and bright it seemed out there and wished to see her dear swallow again. But he never returned. By this time he had flown far away into the lovely green forest.

Then autumn arrived, and Thumbelina's wedding outfit was ready. The field mouse told her, "In four weeks you will marry."

Then Thumbelina wept and said she would not marry the disagreeable mole.

"Nonsense," replied the field mouse. "Don't be stubborn, or I will bite you with my teeth. He is a handsome mole. The queen herself does not wear more beautiful velvets and furs. His kitchen and cellars are full of food. You ought to be thankful for such good fortune."

All too soon, the terrible wedding day came when the mole was to fetch Thumbelina away to live with him, deep under the ground, never again to see the warm sun because he did not like it. The poor girl was heartbroken at the thought of saying farewell to the beautiful sun. Since the field mouse had given her permission to stand in the doorway, she went out to look at the sun for the last time.

"Farewell, bright sun," she cried, reaching out her arm towards the sky. Then she walked a short distance from the house, for the corn had been cut, and only the dry stubble remained. "Farewell, farewell," she repeated, hugging a little red flower that stood by her side. "Greet the little swallow from me, if you should see him again."

"Tweet, tweet," sounded over her head. She looked up, and there was the swallow himself flying by. As soon as he spied Thumbelina, he was overjoyed. She told him that she did not want to marry the dull mole, for that meant she would live beneath the ground and never see the bright sun again. As she told him, she cried many tears.

"The cold winter is coming," said the swallow, "and I am going to fly south. Why not go with me? You can sit on my back and fasten yourself on with your sash. Then we can fly away from the mole and his dark, gloomy rooms—far away, over the mountains to warmer countries. We will go where the sun shines more brightly than here—where it is *always* summer, and where flowers bloom in great beauty. Fly away with me now, dear little Thumbelina. It is the least I can do for you. You saved my life when I lay frozen in that dark tunnel."

"Yes, I will go with you," said Thumbelina delightedly. She seated herself on the bird's back, with her feet on his outstretched wings, and tied herself to one of his strongest feathers.

Then the swallow rose into the air and flew over forest and over sea, high above the highest mountains, covered with deep snow. Thumbelina would have frozen in the cold air, but she snuggled under the bird's warm feathers. She kept her head uncovered though, so she could admire the beautiful lands below.

After a long time they reached warm countries where the sun shines brightly and rises so much higher above the earth. Here, on the hedges and by the roadside, grew purple, green, and white grapes. Lemons and oranges hung from trees, and the air was fragrant with myrtles and orange blossoms. Beautiful children ran along country lanes, chasing after bright-colored butterflies. As the swallow flew farther and farther south, every place they passed seemed still more lovely.

At last they came to a bright blue lake. By the side of it, shaded by trees of the deepest green, stood a palace of dazzling white marble, built a long time ago. Vines clustered around its lofty pillars and at the top were many swallows' nests. One of these was the winter home of the swallow who carried Thumbelina.

"This is my home," said the swallow. "But it would not do for you to live there—you would not be comfortable so high in the air. You must choose one of these lovely flowers, and I will put you down on it.

Then you will have everything that you can wish for to make you happy."

"That will be wonderful," she said and clapped her tiny hands joyfully.

A large marble pillar lay on the ground, which, in falling, had broken into three pieces. Between these pieces grew the most beautiful large white flowers. So the swallow flew down with Thumbelina and placed her on one of the flower's broad leaves. How surprised she was to see in the middle of the flower, a tiny little man, as white and transparent as if he had been made of the finest glass! He had a gold crown on his head, delicate wings attached to his shoulders, and was not much larger than Thumbelina herself. He was, in fact, the angel of that flower. For a tiny man and a tiny woman lived in every flower in that land. This little man was the king of them all.

"Oh, how handsome he is!" whispered Thumbelina to the swallow.

At first, the little prince was frightened by the bird, who was a giant compared to a little one such as himself. But when he saw Thumbelina, he was delighted and thought she was the prettiest little maiden he had ever seen in his entire life. He took the gold crown from his head and placed it on her head. He then asked her name, and if she would agree to be his wife, as well as become queen over all the flowers.

This certainly was a very different kind of husband than an ugly toad who could not talk or a dull mole who hated the sun, so she quickly said, "Yes" to the handsome little prince.

Then all the flowers opened, and out of each came a little lady or a tiny lord, all so pretty that it was a delight to look at them. Each of them brought Thumbelina a present. But the best gift of all was a pair of beautiful wings that once belonged to a large white fly. They fastened them to Thumbelina's shoulders, so she might fly from flower to flower just like them.

Then it was time for the wedding celebration. The little swallow who sat above them in his nest was asked to sing a wedding song, which he did as best he could. But in his heart he was sad. For he was fond of Thumbelina and would have liked never to part from her again.

"You must not be called Thumbelina any more," the spirit of the flowers said to her. "It is such an ugly name, and you are so very pretty. We will call you Maia."

"Farewell, farewell," said the swallow, with a heavy heart, as he left the warm countries to fly back to Denmark the next spring. There he had a nest over the window of a house in which a writer of fairy tales lived. To that writer the swallow sang, "Tweet, tweet." And from his song came this entire story.

4. The Little Mermaid

*A quiet and deeply thoughtful mermaid risks all for true love
and eternal life and wins the better of what she seeks.
Reading time: 1 hour, 15 minutes, 4 parts. All ages.*

Far out in the ocean, where the water is as blue as the prettiest cornflower and as clear as crystal glass, it is very, very deep. So deep, in fact, that the longest rope could not stretch from the top of the water to the bottom of the sea. Nor would many church steeples, stacked one on top of another, reach from the ground beneath to the surface above. That is where the Sea King and his subjects lived.

We must not imagine that there is nothing at the bottom of the sea but bare yellow sand. No indeed! The most unusual flowers and plants grow there, the leaves and stems of which are so flexible that the slightest movement in the water causes them to stir. Fishes, large and small, glide between the branches like birds fly among trees on land.

In the deepest spot of all stands the castle of the Sea King. The castle's walls are made of coral and its windows of the clearest amber. The roof is made from beautiful shells that open and close as the water flows over them. In each lies a glittering pearl that would be fit for the crown of a queen.

"When you have reached your fifteenth year," the Sea King's mother said to her granddaughters, "you may climb out of the sea and sit on the rocks in the moonlight while the great ships sail by. Then for the first time you will see the forests and towns of land."

The following year, the first of six sisters turned fifteen. But as each was a year younger than the other, the youngest would have to wait five long years before her turn came to swim up from the bottom of the ocean to see the surface as we do. However, each sister promised to tell the others what she saw on her first visit, as well as what she thought was the most beautiful. For their grandmother could not tell them enough, and there were so many things they wanted to know about the places where you and I live.

None of them longed as much for her turn to come as the youngest. It was she who had the longest to wait, and it was she who was the most quiet and thoughtful. Many nights she stood by an open window, looking up through the dark blue water and watching the fish as they splashed about with their fins and tails. She could see the moon and stars shining faintly above. Through the water they looked larger than they do to our eyes. When something like a black cloud passed between her and the sky, she knew it was either a whale swimming over her head or a ship filled with people. The people above never imagined that a little mermaid was under them, holding up her hands to the bottom of their ship.

As soon as the eldest was fifteen, she was allowed to swim to the surface. When she came back, she had hundreds of things to describe. But the most beautiful, she said, was to lie in the moonlight on a sandbank in the quiet sea near the coast and gaze at a great city, where the lights twinkled like hundreds of stars You could listen to the sounds of the music, the noise of carriages, and the voices of people. You could even hear merry bells ring out from the church steeples.

Because the youngest sister could not see all those wonderful things, she longed for them more than ever. Oh, how eagerly she listened to those words! Later, when she stood at the open window of her room, looking up through the dark blue water, she thought of the great city, with all its bustle and noise. She even fancied she could hear the sound of church bells deep down in the depths of the sea.

Another year passed, and the second sister received permission to rise to the surface and swim about as she pleased. She rose just as the sun was setting, and this, she said, was the most beautiful sight of all. The whole sky looked like gold, while violet and rose-colored clouds, which she could not describe, floated over her head. A large flock of wild swans flew rapidly toward the setting sun and looked like a long white veil across the sky. She swam toward the sun, but it sank into the waves. Then all the rosy tints faded from the clouds and the sea.

The third sister's turn came the next year. She was the boldest of all and swam up a wide river that emptied into the sea. On its banks she saw green hills covered with beautiful vines. Palaces and castles peeped out from the tall trees of the forest. She heard birds singing, and the rays of the sun were so strong that she often had to dive under the water to cool her burning face.

In a narrow creek she found some little children, quite naked, playing in the water. She wanted to play with them, but they fled in fright when she came close. Then a little black animal came down to the water. It was a dog, but she did not know that for she had never seen one before. It barked at her so fiercely, that she became frightened and swam quickly back to the open sea. But she said she would never forget the beautiful forest, the green hills, and the pretty little children who could swim in the water, although they did not have a fish's tail.

The fourth sister was more timid. She remained in the middle of the sea, but said it was as beautiful there as near land. She could see for many miles around, and the sky above was like a glass bell. She saw ships, but at such a distance that they were like seagulls. The dolphins leaped out of the waves, and great whales spouted until it seemed as if a hundred water fountains were playing in every direction.

The fifth sister's birthday came in winter. When her turn came, she saw what the others had not seen. The sea was very green, and large icebergs floated about. Each was white like a pearl, she said, but larger and taller than the churches built by men. They were of the most unusual shapes and glittered like diamonds. She seated herself on one of the largest and let the wind play with her long hair. She noticed that the ships sailed rapidly by and steered as far as possible away from the iceberg, as if they were afraid of it.

As the sun went down, dark clouds covered the sky, the thunder rolled, the lightning flashed, and the red light of the setting sun glowed on the icebergs as they rocked and tossed on the rolling sea. On all the ships the sailors were so afraid that sails were reduced to their smallest possible size. But she sat calmly on her floating iceberg, watching the blue lightning as it darted its forked flashes into the sea.

When each of the oldest five sisters first got permission to swim to the surface, they were delighted with the new and beautiful sights they saw. But as grown-up women they could now go when they pleased, and soon they cared little for the world above. They preferred to stay under the water with their friends. After a month or so of going to the surface, they said it was much more beautiful down below and pleasanter to be at home.

Yet often in the evening, the oldest five sisters would wrap their arms around each other and rise to the surface in a row. They had more beautiful voices than any human being could possibly have. Before the approach of a storm in which a ship might be lost, they found a ship, swam in front of it, and sang sweetly of the delights to be found in the depths of sea, begging the sailors not to fear if they sank to the bottom. But the sailors could not understand their song and took it for the howling of the storm. Besides, the things the sister sang about were never wonderful for them. If their ship sank, the men would drown and only their dead bodies would reach the palace of the Sea King.

When the sisters rose, arm-in-arm, through the water, their youngest sister was forced stand all alone, looking after them. She would have cried, but mermaids shed no tears, which means they suffer all the more. "Oh, if I were just fifteen years old," she said. "I know I will love the world up there and all the people in it."

The Littlest Mermaid Reaches Fifteen

At last the littlest mermaid reached her fifteenth birthday. "Now you are grown up," said the dowager queen, who was the mother of the king and her grandmother, "you must let me dress you up just like your sisters." The grandmother placed a wreath of white lilies in her hair and in each flower was half a pearl. Then the old lady ordered eight great oysters to attach themselves to the tail of the princess to show her high rank.

"But they hurt so much," cried the little mermaid.

"Pride must suffer pain," replied the old lady. Oh, how gladly the youngest daughter would have shaken off all this grandeur and put aside the heavy wreath around her head! The red flowers in her own garden would have suited her better. But she could not change this, so she said, "Farewell," and rose as lightly as a bubble to the surface of the water.

The sun had just set as she raised her head above the waves. But the clouds were tinted crimson and gold. Through the glimmering twilight shown Venus, the evening star, in all its beauty. The sea was calm, and the air mild and fresh. A large ship with three masts lay becalmed on the water, with only one small sail set. Not a breeze stirred, and the sailors sat idle on deck or among the rigging above the ship. There was music and song on board. As darkness came, a hundred colored lanterns were lit and beautiful flags waved in the air.

Feeling bold, the little mermaid swam close to the cabin windows. Now and then, when the waves lifted her up, she could look in through the clear glass and see the well-dressed people inside. Among them was the most handsome of all, a young prince with large black eyes. He was sixteen years of age, just one year older than the princess, and his birthday was being celebrated. The sailors were dancing on deck. When the prince came out of the cabin, more than a hundred rockets rose into the air, making the sky as bright as day.

The little mermaid was so surprised by the fireworks that she dove under the water. When she put her head up again, it looked as if all the stars of heaven were falling around her. She had never seen such fireworks before. Great suns spurted fire about, splendid fireflies flew into the air, and all their light reflected off the calm sea beneath. The ship itself was so brightly lit that the people and everything on the ship, down to the smallest rope, could be plainly seen. How handsome the young prince looked as he shook the hands of all present and smiled at them, while music rang out through the clear night air.

It was very late, but the little mermaid could not take her eyes off the ship and especially the handsome prince. The colored lanterns had been put away, no more rockets rose into the air, and the cannon had stopped firing. Soon the sea became restless, and a moaning, grumbling sound could be heard beneath the waves. Still the little mermaid remained by the cabin windows, rocking up and down on the water, looking inside.

After a while, the sails were unfurled, and the giant ship began to move again. But soon the waves rose higher, heavy clouds darkened the sky, and lightning flashed in the distance. A dreadful storm was approaching. The sails were made small to prepare for high wind, and the great ship began to fly over the raging sea. The waves rose as high as mountains and reached far above the ship's mast. But the ship dove like a swan between them and then rose again on their lofty, foaming crests. To the little mermaid this appeared to be fun, but it was not that way for the sailors on board. They were very afraid.

After a time, the ship began to groan and creak. The thick planks gave way under the beating of the sea breaking on the deck. Even worse, the thick, towering mainmast snapped in two like a thin reed. Then the ship lay on her side with water pouring in.

The little mermaid realized that the crew was in great danger. Even she had to be careful to avoid the beams and planks of the wreck which lay scattered about in the water. It was so dark that she could not see a single thing. Then a flash of lightning revealed the whole scene. She could see everyone who had been on board except the prince. When the ship had broken in half, she had seen him sink into the waves. At first, she was glad, for that meant he would now be with her. Then she remembered that people could not live under the water. If he sank down to her father's palace, he would be dead.

But he must not die! Desperately, she swam among the beams and planks, forgetting that they could crush her to death. But she could not find the prince. Finally, she saw him! He was growing tired and starting to sink beneath the stormy sea. His arms and legs were failing him, and his beautiful eyes were closed. He would have died if the little mermaid had not come to his assistance. She held his head above the water and let the waves push and toss them where they would.

In the morning the storm had stopped. Not a single piece of the ship could be seen. The sun rose red and glowing from the water. Its rays brought back the color of health to the prince's cheeks, but his eyes remained closed. The mermaid kissed his high, smooth forehead and stroked back his wet hair. To her, he looked like the marble statue in her little garden. She kissed him again and wished he might live.

Soon they were in sight of land. She saw lofty mountains on the which the white snow rested like a flock of swans. Near the coast were beautiful green forests and close by stood a large building. She could not tell whether it was a church or a convent for nuns. Orange and citron trees grew in the garden and before its door stood tall palms.

The sea had created a little bay in which the water was still but deep. She swam with the handsome prince to a beach covered with fine, white sand. There she laid him in the warm sunshine, taking care to raise his head higher than his body. Then bells sounded in the large white building, and some young girls came into the garden. The little mermaid swam out from the shore and hid herself behind some high rocks that rose from the water. She covered her head and neck with the foam of the sea, so her face would not be seen, and watched to see what would become of the sleeping prince.

Soon she saw a young girl approach where he lay. The young girl seemed frightened at first, but only for a moment. Then the girl ran and brought a number of others. The mermaid saw the prince wake up and smile at those who stood around him. But to her he sent no smile. He did not even know she had saved his life. That made her very sad. When he was led away into the great building, she dove under the water. Filled with sorrow, she swam back to her father's castle.

She had always been quiet and thoughtful, but now she was more so than ever. Her sisters asked her what she had seen during her first visit to the surface, but she told them nothing. Many an evening and morning she swam to the place where she had last seen the prince. She saw the fruits in the garden ripen until they were harvested in the fall. Later, she saw the snow on the mountains melt away in the spring. But she did not see the prince again. After each visit, she would return home sadder than ever.

Her only comfort was to sit in her little garden and put her arm around the beautiful marble statue that was so much like the prince. But she gave up tending her flowers. They grew wildly over the paths, wrapping their long leaves and stems around the branches of the trees, so that the whole place became dark and gloomy. Finally, she could stand it no longer and told one of her sisters what had happened. The other sisters soon heard her secret. After that it became known to two mermaids, whose close friend happened to know who the prince was. The friend had also seen the party on the ship and told them where the prince came from and where his palace was.

"Come, little sister," said the other princesses. They joined hands and rose in a long row to the surface of the water, close to the spot where the prince's palace stood. It was made of bright yellow stones, with long flights of marble steps, one of which reached down to the sea. Splendid golden towers rose over the roof. Between the pillars that surrounded the building stood life-like marble statues. Through the clear crystal of the tall windows could be seen rooms with costly silk curtains and hangings of tapestry. Inside, the walls were covered with beautiful paintings. At the center of the largest ballroom, a fountain threw its sparkling jets of water high up in a glass dome, through which the sun shone down on the beautiful plants growing around the fountain. It was a beautiful sight.

Now that she knew where he lived, the little mermaid spent many evenings on the water near the palace. She would swim much nearer to shore than the others dared. Once she went up the narrow channel under a marble balcony, which threw a shadow on the water. There she watched the young prince, who thought he was all alone in the bright moonlight. She saw him many times in the evening, sailing in a beautiful boat with music playing and flags waving. She peeped out from among the green rushes. If the wind caught her long silvery-white veil, those who saw it thought they saw a swan spreading its wings.

On many a night, when the fishermen with their torches were out at sea, she heard them say many good things about the young prince. That made her happy she had saved his life when he had been tossed about in the storm. She remembered how his head had rested on her shoulder, and how eagerly she had kissed him. But he knew nothing of this and could not even dream of her.

Over time, she grew more and more fond of people and wanted to travel with those whose world seemed so much bigger than her own. They could fly over the sea in ships and climb hills far above the clouds. The lands they owned, their forests and their fields, stretched far out of sight. There was so much that she wished to know, and her sisters were unable to answer all her questions. Then she asked her old grandmother, who knew all about the upper world, which she called the lands above the sea.

"If human beings don't drown," asked the little mermaid, "can they live forever? Will they never die like we do here in the sea?"

"No," replied her grandmother, "they also die, and their life is even shorter than ours. We sometimes live three hundred years. But when we cease to exist, we become no more than foam on the surface of the sea. We do not even have a grave down here for those we love. You see, we have no immortal souls. We will never live again. Like the green seaweed when it has been cut off, we have only one brief life.

Human beings are different. Inside they have a soul that lives forever. It lives even after their body has turned to dust. After death it rises up through the clear, pure air to a place far beyond the glittering stars. As we rise out of the water and see all the lands of the earth, so they rise to unknown and wonderful places we will never see."

"Why don't we have an immortal soul?" asked the mermaid sadly. "I would gladly give all the hundreds of years I live to be a human for only one day and enjoy that wonderful world above the stars."

"You must not think of that," said her grandmother. "We believe we are much happier and better off than they."

"So I shall die," said the little mermaid, "and as the foam of the sea I will be driven about, never again to hear the music of the waves or see the pretty flowers or the setting sun. Is there anything I can do to win an immortal soul?"

"No," said her grandmother, "unless a man loves you so much that you mean more to him than his father or mother. If all his thoughts and all his love are centered on no one but you. And if a minister places his right hand in yours, and he promises to be faithful to you now and forever after. Then his soul will enter your body and you will obtain a share in the future happiness of mankind. He will have given you a soul but kept his own as well. But that can never happen. Your fish's tail, which among us is considered beautiful, is thought on land to be quite ugly. They do not know better. They think it necessary to have two stout props, which they call legs, in order to be attractive."

Then the little mermaid sighed, and looked sadly at her fish's tail. "Let us be happy," said the grandmother, "and swim happily about during the three hundred years we are given to live, which is really quite long. After that we can go to our rest all the better. Now don't forget, this evening we are to have a royal ball."

The Fateful Decision

Now a royal ball under the sea is one of those splendid sights that we never see here on land. The walls and the ceiling of the large ballroom are of thick but transparent crystal. Many hundreds of colossal shells, some of a deep red, others of a grass green, stand on each side in rows with blue fire in them. They light up the whole ballroom and shine through the walls, so that the sea is also lit. Uncountable numbers of fishes, great and small, swim past the crystal walls. On some of them, the scales glow with a purple light. On others, they shine like silver and gold. Through the halls flows a broad stream, and in it dances the mermen and the mermaids to their own sweet singing. No one on land has such a lovely voice as they. There, the little mermaid sang more sweetly than them all. The whole court applauded her. For a moment her heart felt quite happy, for she knew she had the loveliest voice of any in the sea or on land.

But she soon thought of the world above her. It seemed that she could never forget the charming prince or the sorrow that she did not have an immortal soul like his. She slipped silently out of her father's palace. While everything within was gladness and song, she sat in her little garden, all sad and alone.

Then she heard a bugle sounding through the water, and thought, "He must be sailing above, the very one on whom all my wishes depend, and in whose hands I would like to place the happiness of my life. I will risk all for him and for an immortal soul. While my sisters are dancing in father's palace, I will go to the terrible Sea Witch and see if she can help me."

So, the little mermaid went out of her garden and took the road to the foaming whirlpools, beyond which the sorceress lived. She had never been that way before. That was not surprising. Neither flower nor grass grew there. Nothing but bare, gray, sandy ground stretched out to the whirlpools. There the water, like foaming mill wheels, whirled around, and everything it seized was tossed into the bottomless deep. Through the middle of those crushing whirlpools, the little mermaid had to pass to reach the Sea Witch.

Once that was passed, for a long distance the only road lay across a warm, bubbling muck, which the Sea Witch called her turf-moor. Beyond that stood her house at the center of a strange forest in which all the trees and flowers looked dreadful, like serpents with a hundred heads. Their branches were long slimy arms with fingers like flexible worms. All that floated in the sea, they grabbed and held fast. Once caught, nothing could escape their clutches.

The little mermaid was so terrified by what she saw, that she stood still, and her heart beat loudly with fear. She almost turned back. Then she thought of the prince and of the human soul for which she longed. Her courage returned. She fastened her long flowing hair around her head, so the forest creatures could not seize it. She lay her arms across her chest, close to her body. Then she darted forward as a fish shoots through the water. She dashed quickly between the supple arms and fingers of the evil creatures that were reaching out their arms on either side of her. She saw that each held in its grasp something it had seized with its many arms, which were like iron bands. There were the white skeletons of human beings who had perished at sea and sunk into the deep water. Oars, rudders, and chests of ships were also tightly grasped by their powerful, clinging arms. There was even a little mermaid that they had caught and strangled. That was the most frightening of all.

At last she came to a patch of marshy ground where large water snakes were rolling about in the mud. In the middle stood a house made from the bones of shipwrecked human beings. Next to it sat the Sea Witch, allowing a toad to eat from her mouth, just like people feed a canary with a piece of sugar. She called the water snakes her little chickens and allowed them to crawl all over her.

"I know what you want," cackled the Sea Witch. "It is very foolish of you, but you will have it your way, though it will bring you much sorrow, my pretty princess. You want to get rid of your fish tail. You want to have two supports, like human beings on land, so the young prince will fall in love with you, and you will have an immortal soul."

Then the Sea Witch laughed so loudly and disgustingly, that the toad and the snakes fell to the ground. "You are just in time," said the Sea Witch. "After sunrise tomorrow, I would not be able to help you until the end of another year. I will prepare a magic potion for you. Then you must swim to land tomorrow before sunrise, sit down on the shore, and drink it. Your tail will shrink to what humans call legs. You will feel great pain, as if a sword were cutting through you. But all who see you will say that you are the prettiest little human being they have ever seen. You will still have your graceful movement. No dancer will ever tread so lightly. But every step you take will feel like you are walking on sharp knives and cause your feet to bleed. If you can bear that, I will help you."

"Yes, I will," said the little princess in a trembling voice, thinking of the prince and of an immortal soul.

"But think again," said the Sea Witch, "for when once your shape has become like a human being, you can never be a mermaid again. You can never return to your sisters or to your father's palace again. If you do not win the love of the prince, so that he is willing to forget his father and mother for your sake, to love you with his whole soul, and to allow a minister to join your hands, so you become man and wife, then you will never have an immortal soul. The first morning after he marries another, your heart will break, and you will become no more than the foam on the crest of waves."

"I will do it," said the mermaid, though she was as pale as death.

"But I must be paid also," cackled the Sea Witch, "and it is not a trifle I ask. You have the sweetest voice of any who dwell in the sea. You believe you will be able to charm the prince with it. But this voice you must give to me. The best thing that you possess, I will have for the price of my magic portion. My own blood must be mixed with the portion, so it will be as sharp as a two-edged sword."

"But if you take away my voice," said the little mermaid, "what is left for me?"

"Your beautiful shape, your graceful walk, and your expressive eyes. Surely with those you can capture any man's heart. Well, have you lost your courage? Put out your tongue, so I can cut it off as my payment. Then you can have the magic potion."

"It shall be," said the little mermaid, uttering the last words she would ever say in this world.

Then the Sea Witch placed her pot on the fire, so she could prepare the magic potion.

"Cleanliness is a good thing," said she, scouring the pot with snakes that she tied in a large knot. Then she pricked herself with a knife and let her dark blood drop into the pot. The steam that rose formed itself into such horrible shapes that no one could look at them without terror. Every moment the Sea Witch threw something different into the pot. When it began to boil, the sound was like the screams of a crocodile. But amazingly, when the magic potion was ready, it looked like the clearest water.

"There it is," said the Sea Witch. "It is all done." Then the sorceress took her knife and cut off the mermaid's tongue, so she became speechless and would never again sing so beautifully. "If the creatures with long arms should grab you as you return through the forest," said the Sea Witch, "throw a few drops of this potion on them, and their fingers will be ripped into a thousand pieces." But the little mermaid had no reason to do that, for they sprang back in terror when they caught sight of the glittering potion, which shone in her hand like a twinkling star.

She passed quickly through the forest and marsh, and then between the deadly whirlpools. Returning home, she saw that in her father's palace the torches in the ballroom had been put out, and everyone was asleep. But she did not dare go to her family, for she could no longer speak and was leaving them never to return. She felt as if her heart would break. She slipped into the garden and took a single flower from the flower beds of each of her sisters. Then with her hand, she tossed a thousand kisses toward the palace. Finally, she rose through the dark blue waters to the surface.

The sun had not yet risen when she came within sight of the prince's palace and its beautiful marble steps. But the moon shone clear and bright. The little mermaid climbed up on the steps and drank the magic potion. Just as the Sea Witch had said, it felt as if a two-edged sword was cutting through her tender body. She fainted to the ground and lay as if she were dead.

When the sun rose and shone over the sea, she recovered, and felt a sharp pain. In front of her stood the handsome young prince. He fixed his coal-black eyes on her so earnestly that she glanced down and saw that her fish's tail was gone, and that she had as pretty a pair of legs and feet as any little maiden could have. But she had no clothes, so she wrapped herself in her long, thick hair.

The prince asked her who she was and where she came from. She looked at him quietly and sorrowfully with her deep blue eyes, but could not speak. Every step she took was as the Sea Witch had said. She felt as she were walking on the points of needles or on sharp knives. But she bore it willingly and stepped as lightly by the prince's side as a soap bubble, so much so that he and all who saw her wondered at her graceful swaying movements. She was soon dressed in costly robes of silk and muslin. All agreed that she was the most beautiful creature in the palace. But she could neither speak nor sing.

Beautiful female servants, dressed in silk and gold, stepped forward and sang before the prince and his royal parents. One sang better than all the others, and the prince clapped his hands and smiled at her. This hurt the little mermaid very much. She knew how much more sweetly she could sing once and thought, "If only he only knew that I have given away my voice forever to be with him for this little time."

Next, the servants performed some charming, fairy-like dances to the sound of beautiful music. The little mermaid raised her lovely arms, stood on the tips of her toes, glided over the floor, and danced as no one else had been able to dance. With each moment her beauty became more revealed, and her expressive eyes appealed more directly to the heart than the songs of the servants. Everyone was enchanted, especially the prince, who called her his little orphan girl. She danced again eagerly, to please him, though each time her foot touched the floor it seemed as if she were walking on sharp knives.

The prince asked her to remain with him always, and she received permission to sleep at his door on a velvet cushion. He had a page's uniform made for her, so she could go with him on horseback. They rode together through the sweet-scented forests, where the green branches brushed their shoulders, and the little birds sang among the fresh leaves. She even climbed with the prince to the tops of high mountains. Although her tender feet bled, so her steps were marked in red, she only laughed and followed him until they were so high they could see the clouds beneath them looking like a flock of white birds flying to distant lands. Back at the prince's palace, after all the household was asleep, she would go and sit on the broad marble steps. For it eased her burning feet to bathe them in the cold seawater. Then she thought of all those she had left behind in the deep sea.

One night her sisters came up, arm-in-arm, singing sorrowfully. She waved to them. They recognized her and told her how her disappearance had made them very sad. From that time on, they came to the same place every night. Once she saw in the distance her old grandmother, who had not been to the surface of the sea for many years, and the old Sea King, her father, with his crown on his head. They stretched out their hands towards her, but they did not dare to go as near to land as her sisters.

Tragedy and Success

As the days passed, she loved the prince more and more. But alas, he loved her as he would love a little child. It never came into his head to make her his wife. Yet, unless he married her, she could not receive an immortal soul. On the morning after his marriage to another, she would dissolve into the foam of the sea.

"Do you not love me best?" the eyes of the little mermaid seemed to say when he took her in his arms and kissed her fair forehead.

"Yes, you are dear to me," said the prince. "For you have the best heart, and you are the most devoted to me. You are like a young maiden I once saw, but whom I will never meet again. I was on a ship that was wrecked, and the waves cast me ashore near a holy temple, where several young maidens performed the service. The youngest of them found me on the shore and saved my life. I saw her but twice. She is the only one in the world I could love. But you are like her. You have almost driven her from my mind. She belongs to the holy temple, and good fortune has sent you to me instead. We will never part."

"Oh, he does not know that it was I who saved his life," thought the little mermaid. "I carried him over the sea to the forest where the temple stands. I sat beneath the foam and watched until the humans came to help him. I even saw the pretty maiden he loves better than me." Then the mermaid sighed deeply, but she still could not shed tears. For inside, she was still a mermaid. "He says the maiden belongs to the holy temple, so she will never return to the world," she thought. "That means they will never meet again. While I am by his side and see him every day, I will take care of him, love him, and give up my life for his sake. Maybe he will come to love me as his wife."

Soon afterward, it was rumored that the prince must marry for the sake of the kingdom, and that the beautiful daughter of a neighboring king would be his wife. For that journey, a fine ship was prepared. Although the prince told people he merely intended to pay a visit to the king, it was generally supposed that he really went to see the daughter. A great number of people were to go with him. The little mermaid smiled and shook her head. He would not marry the princess. She knew the prince's thoughts better than anyone else.

"I must travel," he had said to her. "I must see this beautiful princess. My parents desire it. But they will not force me to bring her home as my bride. I cannot love her, for she is not the beautiful maiden in the temple, whom you resemble. If I were forced to choose a bride, I would rather have you, my tongueless orphan girl with such expressive eyes." Then he kissed her rosy mouth, played with her long waving hair, and laid his head on her heart, while she dreamed of human happiness and an immortal soul.

"You are not afraid of the sea, my child," said he, as they stood on the deck of the noble ship that was carrying them to the country of the neighboring king. Then he told her of storm and calm seas, of strange fishes in the deep beneath, and what divers had seen there. She smiled at his description, for she knew better than any human what wonders lay at the bottom of the sea.

In the moonlight, when all on board were asleep except the man at the helm who steered the boat, she sat on the deck, gazing down through the clear water. She thought she could see her father's castle, and on it her aged grandmother, with a silver crown on her head, looking through the rushing sea at the bottom of the ship. Then her sisters came to the surface and gazed at her mournfully, wringing their hands. She waved to them and smiled. She wanted to tell them how happy and well off she was. But a cabin boy approached. When her sisters dove under, he thought it was only the foam of the sea he saw.

The next morning the ship sailed into the harbor of a beautiful town belonging to the king that the prince was to visit. Church bells rang and from high towers trumpets sounded. Soldiers, with their colorful uniforms and glittering bayonets, lined the streets through which they passed. Every day was a festival. Every night there was a party or ball.

But the princess had not yet appeared. People said she was being brought up in a religious house where she was learning every royal virtue. At last she came. Then the little mermaid, who was anxious to see whether she was really beautiful, was obliged to acknowledge that she had never seen a more perfect vision of beauty. Her skin was delicately fair and beneath her long dark eyelashes her laughing blue eyes shone with truth and purity.

"It was you," said the prince, "who saved my life when I lay on the beach," and he folded his blushing bride in his arms. "Oh, I am so happy," he said to the little mermaid. "My fondest hopes are fulfilled. In your devotion, rejoice at my happiness."

The little mermaid kissed his hand. But it felt as if her heart had broken in two. His wedding morning would bring her death as she was changed into the foam of the sea. All the church bells rang, and the heralds rode about proclaiming the engagement. Perfumed oil was burned in costly silver lamps on every altar. The priests waved their good-smelling censers, while the bride and bridegroom joined their hands and received the blessing of the bishop. The little mermaid, dressed in silk and gold, held the train of the bride's dress. But her ears heard none of the beautiful music, and her eyes did not see the holy ceremony. She thought only of the night of death that was coming on her and of all that she had lost.

That same evening the bride and bridegroom went on board the prince's ship. Cannons were roaring, flags waving, and at the center of the ship a costly tent of purple and gold had been set up. It contained elegant couches where the bridal pair would sleep during the night. The ship, with swelling sails and a favorable wind, glided away smoothly and lightly over the calm sea.

When it grew dark, colored lamps were lit, and the sailors danced merrily on deck. The little mermaid could not help thinking of her first rising out of the sea, when she had seen a similar celebration. She joined in the dance, poising herself in the air as light a swallow. All present cheered her with wonder. She had never danced so elegantly. Her tender feet felt as if they had been cut with sharp knives, but she cared not. A sharper pang had pierced her heart.

She knew this was the last evening she would ever see the prince for whom she had forsaken her family and home. She had given up her beautiful voice and suffered unheard-of pain daily for him. But he knew nothing of that. This was the last evening she would breathe the same air with him or gaze on the starry sky and the deep sea. An eternal night, without thought or dream, awaited her. She had no soul and now she could never win one. All was joy and happiness on board the ship until long after midnight. She laughed and danced with the rest, while thoughts of death haunted her heart. The prince kissed his beautiful bride, while she played with his dark hair until they went arm-in-arm to sleep in the splendid tent.

Then all became still on board the ship. The helmsman, alone awake, stood at the helm. The little mermaid leaned her arms on the edge of the vessel and looked to the east for the first blush of morning, for the first ray of dawn would bring her death. Then she saw her sisters rising out of the sea. They were as pale as herself. But their long and beautiful hair waved no more in the wind. It had been cut off.

"We have given our hair to the Sea Witch," said they, "to get help for you, so you will not die tonight. She has given us a knife. Here it is. See, it is very sharp. Before the sun rises you must plunge it into the heart of the prince. When the warm blood falls on your feet, they will grow together again and form a fish's tail. Then you will once more be a mermaid and can return to us to live out your three hundred years before you die and change into sea foam. Hurry! Either he or you must die before the sunrise. Our old grandmother moans so for you that her white hair is falling out from sorrow, as ours fell under the Sea Witch's scissors. Kill the prince and come back. Don't you see the first red streaks in the sky? In a few minutes the sun will rise, and you will die." Then they sighed mournfully and sank beneath the waves.

The little mermaid drew back the crimson curtain of the tent and saw the beautiful bride with her head resting on the prince's chest. She bent down and kissed his fair brow, then looked at the sky where the rosy dawn was growing brighter and brighter. She looked at the sharp knife and again turned her eyes to the prince, who whispered the name of his new bride in his dreams. The princess was in his thoughts, The knife trembled in the hand of the little mermaid. Then she flung it far away from her into the waves. The water turned red where it fell, and the drops that splashed up looked like blood. She cast one more lingering, half-fainting glance at the prince and then threw herself into the sea. She felt as if her body was dissolving into foam.

The sun rose above the waves, and its warm rays fell on the cold foam of the little mermaid, who did not feel as if she were dying. She saw the bright morning sun. All around her were hundreds of beautiful, transparent beings. Through them she could see the white sails of the ship and the red clouds in the sky. Their speech was musical, but too high and heavenly to be heard by mortal ears, as they were also unseen by mortal eyes. The little mermaid saw that she had a body like theirs, and that she was rising higher and higher out of the foam.

"Where am I?" asked she, speaking again for first time. Her voice sounded as heavenly as that of those who were with her. No earthly music could imitate it.

"Among the daughters of the air," answered one of them. "A mermaid does not have an immortal soul, nor can she get one unless she wins the love of a human being. On the power of another hangs her eternal destiny. But the daughters of the air, although they do not have an immortal soul, can, by their good deeds, win one for themselves. We fly to warm countries and cool the hot, humid air that kills mankind with disease. We carry the perfume of flowers to spread health and restoration. After we have worked to do all the good in our power for three hundred years, we receive an immortal soul and join in the happiness of mankind. You, poor little mermaid, have tried with your whole heart to do as we are doing. You have suffered, endured and raised yourself to the spirit world by your good deeds. Now, by striving for three hundred years in the same way, you can get an immortal soul."

The little mermaid lifted her new eyes to the sun and felt them, for the first time, filling with tears. On board the ship where she had left the prince, there was life and activity. She saw him and his beautiful bride searching for her. Sadly, they gazed at the sea foam, as if they knew she had thrown herself into the waves. Unseen, she kissed the forehead of the bride, waved at the prince, and then rose with the other daughters of the air to a rosy cloud that floated in the morning sky.

"After three hundred years like this we will fly into the kingdom of heaven," said one of the daughters of the air.

"And we may even get there sooner," whispered one of her companions. "Unseen we enter houses where there are children. Every time we find a good child, who is the joy of his parents, our time of probation is shortened. The child does not know, when we fly through the room, that we smile with joy at his good conduct, for we can count one year less of our three hundred years. But when we see a naughty or a wicked child, we shed tears of sorrow. For every tear, a day is added to our time of trial!"

—§§§—

5. The Daisy

A humble daisy enjoys the beauty of God in nature and, unnoticed by others, is kind to a bird dying in a cage. Reading time: 13 minutes. All ages.

Out in the country, close to a busy road, stood a farmhouse. Perhaps you have passed by and seen it for yourself. It was a pretty farmhouse. There was even a little flower garden with a white fence in front of it. Close by was a ditch and on its beautiful green bank grew an ordinary little daisy. Yet the sun shone as warmly and brightly on this wild daisy as it did on the magnificent flowers in the garden. As a result, she thrived and grew strong.

Each morning she opened up the snowy white petals that grew around her yellow center just like the rays of the sun. She did not mind in the slightest that no one saw her in the grass, or that she was considered a poor and unimportant little flower. No, she was quite happy to be herself and to be alive. She enjoyed the warm sun and loved listening to the song of a lark high in the air. For this little daisy, everyday life was wonderful.

On one rather ordinary Monday, the daisy was as happy as if she had been a great holiday. All the children were at school. While they sat at their desks and learned their lessons, the daisy sat on her thin green stalk and learned from the sun and nature just how kind God is. She rejoiced that the song of the lark expressed so sweetly her own joy at life. With reverence the daisy looked up at the birds that flew about and sang over her head. But she did not feel the slightest bit of envy. "I can see and hear," she thought. "The sun shines on me, and the forest kisses me. How rich I am!"

In the garden close by grew many large and magnificent flowers. Strange as it sounds, the less fragrance they had, the haughtier and prouder they behaved. The peonies puffed themselves up in order to be larger than the roses, but size is not everything. The tulips had the finest colors. But they knew that all too well and were standing bolt upright like candles on display, so everyone would notice them. It was a sad thing to see.

In their pride none of them noticed the little daisy, who looked over at them and thought, "How rich and beautiful they are! I am sure a pretty bird will fly down and call on them. Thank God, that I stand so near and can at least see them in all their beauty."

While the daisy was thinking that, a lark came flying down, crying "Tweet." But he did not come to the proud peonies and tulips. No, he landed in the grass next to our plain little daisy. Her joy was so great that she did not know what to think.

The little bird hopped around her and sang, "How beautifully soft the grass is, and what a lovely little flower with its golden heart and silver dress is growing here." The yellow center in the daisy did indeed look like gold, and her little petals did shine as brightly as silver.

How happy the daisy was! No one had the least idea just how happy she was. The bird kissed her with his beak, sang to her, and then flew into the blue sky. More than a quarter of an hour passed before the daisy recovered her senses. Half ashamed, yet glad at heart, she looked over at the flowers in the garden. They must have witnessed her pleasure and the honor she had received. They must understand how happy she was. But the tulips stood more stiffly than ever, their faces pointed and red because they were angry and upset. The peonies were sulky. It was good that they could not speak, otherwise they would have given the daisy a stern lecture. The little flower could see that they were ill at ease, and she pitied them sincerely. Why couldn't they just enjoy life and not be so proud and self-centered?

Just after that, a girl came into the garden with a large sharp knife. She went up to the tulips and began cutting them off, one after another. "Ugh!" sighed the daisy, "That is terrible. Now they are done for."

The girl carried the tulips away. The daisy was grateful that she was not in the garden, where she might be cut off, but instead a small and unimportant wildflower that no one noticed. At sunset she folded her petals, fell asleep, and dreamed all night of the sun and of the wonderful little bird who had visited her.

The following morning the flower once more stretched out her tender petals like little arms toward the light and air. Then the daisy recognized the voice of the lark that had visited her the day before. But now his singing was very sad. The poor bird had good reason to be unhappy. He had been caught and put in a cage near an open window. He sang of happy days, when he could merrily fly about, of fresh green corn in the fields, and of the time when he could soar almost to the clouds. The poor lark was as miserable as a prisoner in a cage.

The little daisy would have liked to help. But what could she do for him? That was very difficult for a small flower to know. In her sorrow for someone else, she completely forgot how beautiful everything around her was, how warmly the sun was shining, and how splendidly white her own petals were. In her kindness, she could only think of the poor bird in the cage for whom she could do nothing.

Then two little boys came out of the garden. One of them had a large sharp knife, much like that the girl had used to cut the tulips. They came straight towards the little daisy, who could not understand what they wanted.

"Here is a fine piece of turf for our lark," said one of the boys, and he began to cut a square of grass out around the daisy, so she remained in the center.

"Pluck the flower off," said the other boy. The daisy trembled with fear, for to be plucked meant death for her. She wanted very much to live, especially since she was to go with the square of grass into the poor lark's cage.

"No, let it stay," said the other boy, "it looks pretty."

So she stayed and was brought into the lark's cage. The unfortunate little bird was weeping over his lost freedom and beating his wings against the cage. Since flowers cannot talk, the poor little daisy could not speak or utter a single kind word, much as she would have liked to do so. Then the middle of the day passed and it became warm.

"I have no water," said the lark in the cage, "they have all gone away and forgotten to give me anything to drink. My throat is dry and burning. I feel as if I had fire and ice inside me, and the air is so heavy. Sob, I must die and leave the warm sunshine, the fresh green meadows, and all the beauty God has created." He thrust his beak into the piece of grass, to refresh himself a little. Then he noticed the little daisy, nodded to her, and kissed her once again with his beak. He said, "You must also fade and die in here, poor little flower. You and the piece of grass are all they have given me in exchange for the world I once enjoyed outside. Each little blade of grass will be like a green tree for me, each one of your white petals a fragrant flower. Sob, you remind me of what I have lost."

"I wish I could make the poor lark feel better," thought the little daisy. She could not move even one of her leaves, but the fragrance of her delicate petals streamed out and was much stronger than flowers usually have. The bird noticed that. Although he was dying with thirst and in his pain he tore up the green blades of grass, he did not touch the daisy or do her any harm.

Evening came and still nobody brought the poor bird a drop of water. He opened his wings and fluttered about in anguish. A faint and mournful "Tweet, tweet," was all he could utter, then he bent his little head towards the flower, and his heart broke for want and longing.

When dark came, the daisy did not have the strength to fold up her petals and sleep. Instead, she drooped down sorrowfully. The boys finally came the next morning. When they saw the dead bird, they began to cry bitterly. Then they dug a nice grave for him and decorated it with flowers. The bird's body was put in a pretty red box. They wished to bury him with royal honors, as if he had been a prince.

While the bird was alive and sang, they forgot him and let him suffer in the cage. Now they cried over him and covered him with flowers. The piece of turf with the little daisy in it was thrown out on to the dusty highway. Nobody thought for a moment of the ordinary daisy that had shown so much kindness for the little bird and had tried so hard to comfort him as he was dying in that cage.

—§§§—

6. The Wild Swans

With great courage and a willingness to endure pain and risk death, a sister rescues her eleven brothers from an evil curse.
Reading time: 55 minutes, 3 parts. All ages.

Far away, in a land to where the swallows fly for winter, lived a king who had eleven sons and a daughter named Eliza. The eleven brothers were princes. Each went to school with a golden star on his chest and a sword by his side. They wrote with diamond pencils on golden slates and learned their lessons so quickly and read so easily that every one just knew they had to be princes.

Their sister Eliza sat on a stool made of glass and had a book full of beautiful pictures that had cost half a kingdom. These children were very happy. But it was not to remain that way. No, not at all.

Their mother had died. Their father married a wicked new queen who did not love her stepchildren. They knew this from the very first day after the wedding. In the palace there were great parties, and the children played at their own small party. But instead of having, as usual, all the cakes and apples that were left over, the new queen gave them sand in a teacup and told them to pretend it was cake. The week after that she sent little Eliza into the country to a farmer and his wife. Then she told the king many untrue things about the young princes. The king foolishly believed her and quit trusting his own sons.

"Go out into the world and take care of yourselves," the queen said to her stepsons. "Fly like great birds with no voice," she ordered, for she was secretly a wicked witch. But she could not make them ugly, as she had wanted. Instead, the brothers became eleven beautiful wild swans. Then, with a strange and mournful cry, they flew out the windows of the palace, over the park, and into the forest beyond.

It was early morning when they passed the farmer's cottage where their sister Eliza was asleep in her room. They hovered over the roof, twisted their long necks, and flapped their wings. But no one heard them or saw them, so they were forced to fly on, high up in the clouds. They flew until they came to a dark forest that stretched down to a sea.

Later, we find poor Eliza alone in her room playing with a green leaf, for the family she was living with was so poor that she had no other toys. She pierced a hole in the leaf and looked through it at the sun. Then it seemed as if she saw her brothers' clear eyes. When the warm sun shone on her cheeks, she thought of all the kisses they had once given her. Oh, how she missed them!

For Eliza, one day passed just like any other. Sometimes the winds rustled through the leaves of the rosebush and whispered to the roses, "Who can be more beautiful than you!" But the roses would shake their heads, and say, "Eliza is." When the old woman sat at her cottage door on Sunday and read in her hymn book, the wind would flutter the pages, and say to the book, "Who can be more interested in God than this woman?" Then the hymn book would answer "Eliza." The roses and the hymn book told the truth.

At fifteen she returned home to the palace. But when the queen saw how beautiful Eliza had become, she was filled with spite and hatred. She would have turned Eliza into a swan on the spot just like her brothers. But she did not dare to do that, because the king wished to see his only daughter.

Early one morning the queen went into Eliza's bathroom. It was made of marble and had soft cushions trimmed with beautiful lace. She took three toads with her, kissed them, and said to one, "When Eliza comes into the bath, seat yourself on her head, so she will become as stupid as you are." She said to the second, "Place yourself on her forehead, so she will become as ugly as you, and her father will not know her." "Rest on her heart," she whispered to the third, "so she will have evil desires and suffer terrible consequences." Then she put the three toads into the water, and they all turned green.

Next, the wicked queen called Eliza and helped her to undress and get into the bath. As Eliza dipped her head under the water, one of the toads sat on her hair, a second on her forehead, and a third on her chest.

But she did not notice them. When she rose out of the water, there were three red poppies floating on it.

If the creatures had not been poisonous or if they had not been kissed by the witch, they would have been changed into beautiful red roses. Instead they were transformed into poppies, because they had rested on Eliza's head and on her heart. She was simply too good and too innocent for witchcraft to have any power over her.

When the wicked queen saw this, she rubbed Eliza's face with walnut juice, so she looked very dirty. Then she tangled Eliza's beautiful hair and smeared it with a disgusting ointment until it was impossible to recognize the beautiful young girl.

When her father saw her, he was shocked and claimed that she must not be his daughter. No one but the watchdog and the swallows knew her. But of course they were only poor animals and could say nothing. Then poor Eliza wept and thought of her eleven brothers far away.

Sorrowfully, she slipped away from the palace and walked the whole day across fields and moors until she came to a great forest. She did not know where to go from there. She was so unhappy and longed so much for her brothers. Just like her, they had been driven into the world by the wicked queen. From that moment on, she decided to find them, whatever the cost to her.

She had been only a short time in the forest when night came and she lost the path on which she was traveling. Wisely, before she got even more lost, she lay down on the soft moss, said her evening prayers, and leaned her head against the stump of a tree. All nature was still, and the soft, mild air blew across her forehead in the gentlest of caresses. The light of hundreds of fireflies shone out from the grass and moss like a green fire. If she touched a twig with her hand ever so lightly, the brightly lit insects fell down around her like shooting stars falling from the sky.

All night long she dreamed of her eleven brothers. She remembered when they were children playing together. She saw them writing with their diamond pencils on golden slates, while she looked at the beautiful picture book that had cost half a kingdom. They were not doing schoolwork, as they once did. They were writing tales of the noble deeds they had performed and of all that they had discovered and seen. In her magical picture book everything was alive. The birds sang, and the people came out of the book and spoke to Eliza and her brothers. But, as pages were turned over, they darted back to their places in the story, so everything in the book stayed in order. Wasn't that wonderful?

When she awoke the next morning, the sun was already high in the sky. But she could not see it, for the lofty trees spread their branches thickly over her head. But the sun's beams were peeking through the leaves here and there, like a golden mist. There was a sweet fragrance from the fresh green plants, and the birds were so unafraid of people that they almost perched on her shoulders. She heard water rippling from a number of springs, all flowing into a lake with golden sands. Bushes grew thickly around the lake, and at one place an opening had been made by the deer. Through it Eliza went down to the water.

The lake was so clear that, if the wind had not rustled the branches of the trees and the bushes so that they moved, it would have looked like the scenery had been painted in the depths of the lake. Every leaf was reflected in the water, whether it stood in the shade or the sunshine. As soon as Eliza saw her own face, she was upset to find it looked so dirty. She wet her hand and scrubbed her face to make it clean. Then she undressed and washed herself in the fresh water. Now a more beautiful princess could not be found in the whole wide world.

As soon as she had dressed and braided her long hair, she went to a bubbling spring and drank water using her hand as a cup. Then she went deeper into the forest, not knowing where she was going. She thought constantly of her brothers and felt God would not desert her.

It is God who makes the wild apples grow in the forest to satisfy the hungry. He now led her to one of these trees, which was so loaded with fruit that its branches bent beneath their weight. Here she had lunch. In kindness to the tree, she placed props under its branches, so they would not break from the weight of all those apples.

Finding Eleven Swans

Growing braver, Eliza went into the darkest and gloomiest part of the forest. It was so quiet there that she could hear the sound of her own footsteps and the rustling of every fallen leaf as she stepped on it. Not a bird was seen. Not a single sunbeam penetrated through the dark branches of the trees. Their lofty trunks stood so close together that when she looked in front of her, it seemed as if she were inside a garden fence. In her entire life, she had never been so alone. Night came and it became dark. Not a single firefly glittered in the moss.

Feeling sad, she lay down to sleep. After a while, it seemed as if the tree branches parted over her head, and the warm and kind eyes of angels looked down on her from heaven. It was so amazingly real, that when she awoke the next morning she did not know whether she had been dreaming, or if it had actually happened.

That day she continued her wandering. But she had not gone far before she met an old woman with berries in her basket who gave her a few to eat. Then Eliza asked her if she had seen eleven princes riding through the forest.

"No," replied the old woman, "But yesterday I saw eleven swans with gold crowns on their heads swimming on the river nearby."

She led Eliza a little distance farther to a sloping bank and at the foot of it ran a little river. The trees on its banks stretched their long leafy branches across the water toward each other. Where the growth prevented them from meeting naturally, the roots had torn themselves away from the ground, so the branches might mingle their foliage as they hung out over the water.

Eliza thanked the old woman and wished her goodbye. Then she walked along the river until she reached a seashore. Before her eyes lay a vast ocean. But not a sail appeared on its surface, and not a single boat could be seen. How was she to go any further? She looked down and noticed how the countless pebbles on the seashore had been smoothed and rounded by the action of the water. Glass, iron, stones, everything that lay there mingled together, had taken its shape from the same power and felt as smooth or even smoother than her own soft hands.

"The water rolls on without tiring," she said, "until everything that is hard becomes smooth. In the same way I will never grow weary looking for my brothers. Thank you for your lesson, bright rolling waves. My heart tells me you will lead me to my dear brothers."

On the foam-covered seaweed lay eleven white swan feathers, which she gathered up and placed together. Drops of water lay on them. Whether they were dewdrops or tears no one could say.

It may have been lonely on that seashore, but she did not notice. For the ever-moving sea showed more changes in a few hours than a lake could produce during a whole year. If a black and heavy cloud arose, it was as if the sea had said, "I can look dark and angry." Then the wind blew and the waves turned to white foam as they rolled in. When the wind slept and the clouds glowed with the red sunlight, the sea looked like a rose leaf. But however quietly its white glassy surface rested, there was still a motion on the shore, as its waves rose and fell like the chest of a sleeping child.

Just as the sun was about to set, Eliza saw eleven white swans with golden crowns on their heads flying toward the land, one behind the other like a long white ribbon. She went down and hid herself behind some bushes. Then the swans landed quite close to her and flapped their great white wings.

As soon as the sun had gone down, the feathers of the swans fell off and eleven handsome princes, Eliza's brothers, stood in front of her. She uttered a loud cry, for though they were much changed, she knew them immediately. She sprang into their arms and called each by name. How happy the princes were to meet their little sister again. Although she had grown tall and beautiful, they recognized her too. Together the sister and brothers laughed and wept. Soon they discovered how wickedly their stepmother had treated them.

"We brothers," said the eldest, "fly about as wild swans as long as the sun is in the sky. But as soon as it sinks behind the hills, we recover our human shape. That means must we always find a resting place for our feet before sunset. For if we are flying in the clouds when we recover our natural shape as men, we would fall into the sea. We do not live here. We live in a beautiful land beyond the ocean. To visit here, we cross many miles of ocean, and there is no island on which we can spend the night. There is only a little rock rising out of the sea, on which we can barely stand, even closely crowded together. If the sea is rough, the foam dashes over us. Yet we thank God for that little rock— we have spent entire nights clinging to it. Without it, we could never reach our beloved homeland. For our flight across the sea fills two of the longest days of the year.

We have permission to visit out home once every year and to remain eleven days, during which we fly across the forest to look once more at our father's palace, at the place where we were born, and at the church where our mother lies buried. Here it seems as if the very trees and bushes are related to us. The wild horses leap over the plains as we saw them in our childhood. The charcoal burners sing the old songs to which we danced as children. This is our homeland, the one to which we are drawn by loving ties. Now we have found you, our dear little sister. In two days must we fly back to a beautiful land that is not our own. But how can we take you with us? We have no ship to sail."

"How can I break this evil spell?" asked their sister. She talked with them about it almost the entire night, only sleeping for a few hours. As the sun came up, Eliza was awakened by the rustling of the swans' wings as they soared above her. Her brothers had been changed back into swans, and they flew in wider and wider circles, until they were far away. But one of them, the youngest, remained behind. He laid his head in his sister's lap, while she stroked his wings. They remained together the whole day. Near evening the rest came back, and, as the sun went down, they resumed their human shape.

"Tomorrow," said one, "we must fly away and not return until a whole year has passed. But we cannot leave you here. Have you enough courage to go with us? My arm is strong enough to carry you through the forest. Perhaps together all our wings will be strong enough to carry you over the sea?"

"Yes, take me with you," said Eliza without hesitation.

They spent the whole night weaving a net from flexible willow branches and the leaves of rushes. It was large and strong. Then Eliza lay down on the net and went to sleep. When the sun rose the next morning, her brothers again became wild swans. They took the net up in their beaks and flew into the clouds with their dear sister still sleeping. To keep the sunbeams from falling on her face, one of the swans flew over her head and used his broad wings to shade her.

They were far from land when Eliza awoke. She thought she must still be dreaming. It seemed strange to feel herself being carried high in the air. By her side lay a branch full of ripe berries and a bundle of sweet roots. The youngest of her brothers had gathered them for her and placed them by her side. She smiled her thanks to him. He was the one who shaded her with his wings.

They were now so high up that a large ship beneath them looked no bigger than a white seagull skimming the waves. A great cloud floating behind them appeared like a huge mountain. On it Eliza saw her own shadow and those of the eleven swans, looking gigantic in size. It was the most beautiful picture she had ever seen. But as the sun rose higher and the clouds were left behind, their shadows vanished.

The whole day they flew on like a winged arrow, yet more slowly than usual, for they had their sister to carry. The weather was also stormy, and Eliza watched the sinking sun with anxiety. For the one little rock they could rest on in that vast ocean was not yet in sight. She could see that her swan brothers making great efforts with their wings to reach it. Alas! She was the reason they were flying so slowly. When the sun set, they would change into men, fall into the sea, and drown.

She offered a prayer from her inmost heart, but the rock still did not appear. Dark clouds came nearer and gusts of wind told of a coming storm, while from a thick, heavy mass of clouds the lightning burst in flash after flash. The sun was already touching the edge of the sea when the swans darted down so swiftly that Eliza's head trembled. She believed they were falling, but they continued to fly on.

Finally, she caught sight of the rock just below them. By this time the sun was half hidden by the waves. The rock seemed no larger than a seal's head thrust out of the water. The swans dropped down rapidly and, at the moment their feet touched the rock, the sun was no larger than a tiny star on the horizon. Seconds later, it disappeared like the last spark in a piece of burnt paper.

Eliza's brothers stood closely around her with their arms linked. There was no room to spare. The sea dashed against the rock, and covered them with spray. The heavens were lit with flashes of lightning, and peal after peal of thunder rolled across the sky. But the sister and brothers sat holding each other's hands and singing the hymns they had learned as children and from which they drew hope and courage. In the early dawn the air became calm and still. At sunrise the swans flew away from the rock with Eliza. The sea was still rough, and from high in the air the white foam on the dark green waves looked like millions of swans swimming over the water.

As the sun rose higher, Eliza saw, floating in the air in front of her, what seemed to be a range of mountains, with shining ice on their summits. In the center, rose a castle a mile long with rows of columns, rising one above another. Around it palm trees waved and giant flowers bloomed. She asked if this was the land to which they were going. The swans shook their heads. What she saw, they said, were the beautiful and ever-changing cloud palaces of "Fata Morgana," into which no mortal can enter.

Eliza was gazing at the scene when the mountains, forests and castles melted away, and twenty stately churches arose, with high towers and pointed gothic windows. Eliza even imagined she could hear the tones of an organ, but it was only the murmuring sea.

As they drew nearer to the churches, they changed into a fleet of ships, which seemed to be sailing beneath her. But as she looked again, she found it was only the sea mist gliding over the ocean.

All day, constant changing scenes passed before her eyes, until at last she saw the real land to which they were bound, with its blue mountains, cedar forests, cities and palaces. Long before the sun went down, she sat on a rock in front of a large cave, on the floor of which the overgrown yet delicate green creeping plants looked like an embroidered carpet. "Now we wait to hear what you will dream tonight," said the youngest brother, as he showed his sister her bedroom in the cave.

"May heaven grant I dream of a way to save you," she answered.

Rescuing Her Brothers

This thought took such hold of her mind that she prayed earnestly to God for help, so earnestly that even in her sleep she continued to pray. In her dream it appeared as if she were flying high in the air toward the cloudy palace of the "Fata Morgana." A fairy came out to meet her, radiant and beautiful. Yet she looked very much like the old woman who had given her berries in the wood and told her of the swans with golden crowns on their heads. Had she come again?

"Your brothers can be released from the curse," said the fairy, "if you have courage and perseverance. True, water is softer than your own delicate hands, and yet it polishes stones into shapes. But water feels no pain as your fingers will feel. It has no soul and cannot suffer the agony and torment you must endure. Do you see the stinging nettle that I hold in my hand? Nettles like it grow all around the cave in which you sleep. But none will be of any use unless they grow on the graves of a churchyard. These you must gather even when they burn blisters on your hands. Break them into pieces with your bare hands and feet. They will become flax from which you must spin and weave eleven coats with long sleeves. If these are thrown over the eleven swans, the spell will be broken. But remember, from the moment you start your task until it is finished—even should it take years—you must not speak a single word. The first word you utter will pierce through your brother's hearts like a deadly dagger. Their lives depend on your tongue. Remember all that I have told you." As she finished speaking, she touched Eliza's hand lightly with the nettle. A pain like burning fire awoke Eliza.

It was broad daylight, and close to where she had been sleeping lay a nettle like the one she had seen in her dream. She fell on her knees and thanked God. Then she went out of the cave to begin work with her delicate hands. She pulled up the ugly nettles, which burned great blisters on her hands and arms. But she was determined to bear it gladly to free her dear brothers. Then she bruised the nettles with her bare feet and spun the flax, again in great pain.

At sunset her brothers returned and were frightened when they found her unable to speak. They believed it was some new sorcery by their wicked stepmother. But when they saw her hands they understood what she was doing for them. The youngest brother wept and, when his tears fell on her hands and feet, the pain ceased and the burning blisters vanished.

She kept to her work all night, for she did not want to rest a moment until she had made all eleven coats and released her dear brothers from the evil spell. During the whole of the following day, while her brothers were absent, she worked alone. But so great was her eagerness that never had time passed so quickly for her.

One coat was already finished and she had begun the second, when she heard a hunter's horn and was struck with fear. The sound came nearer and nearer. She heard dogs barking and fled terrified into the cave. She quickly bound together the nettles she had gathered into a bundle and sat on them.

Soon a great hunting dog came leaping toward her out of the ravine, then another, and yet another. They barked loudly, ran back the hunters, and returned again. In a few minutes all the hunters stood in front of the cave. The handsomest of them was the king of the country. He came up to her smiling, for he had never seen a more beautiful young woman.

"How did you come here, my sweet child?" he asked. But Eliza shook her head. She dared not speak, at the cost of her brothers' lives. She hid her hands under her apron, so the king would not see how badly she was suffering.

"Come with me," he said. "You cannot live in this rough cave. It is not healthy. If you are as good as you are beautiful, I will dress you in silk and velvet and place my golden crown on your head. You will rule as queen and make your home in my finest castle." Then he lifted her on his horse.

She wept and wrung her hands in sorrow, but the king said, "I only want your happiness. The time will come when you will thank me for this."

Then the king galloped away over the mountains, holding her in front of him on his horse, with the other hunters following behind. As the sun went down, they approached a beautiful royal city, with churches and high towers.

Arriving at his castle the king led her into marble halls where large fountains flowed and where the walls and ceilings were covered with beautiful paintings. But she had no eyes for these wonderful sights. She could only mourn and weep for the brothers she had left behind.

Patiently, she allowed the women to dress her in royal robes, to weave pearls in her hair, and draw soft gloves over her blistered hands. As she stood before them in her rich dress, she looked so dazzlingly beautiful that the court bowed low. Then the king announced his intention to make her his bride. But the archbishop shook his head and whispered that the fair young maiden was a witch who had blinded the king's eyes and bewitched his heart.

The king would not listen to this. He ordered music to be played, the daintiest dishes to be served, and the loveliest maidens to dance. Afterward he led her through fragrant gardens and lofty halls. But not the tiniest smile appeared on her lips or sparkled in her eyes. She was the very picture of grief.

Then the king opened the door of a little chamber in which she was to sleep. It was decorated with rich green tapestry, but it also resembled the cave in which he had found her. On the floor lay the bundle of flax that she had spun from the nettles and from the ceiling hung the one coat she had made. They had been brought from the cave as curiosities by one of the hunters.

"Here you can dream your are back in your old home in the cave," said the king. "Here is the work you did then. In the midst of all this splendor, it may amuse you to remember that terrible time."

When Eliza saw all the things that were so dear to her heart, a smile came to her face, and red blood rushed to her cheeks. She thought of her brothers. The thought of their release made her so happy that she kissed the king's hand. Then he pressed her to his heart.

Soon, joyous church bells announced that the beautiful girl from the forest who could not speak was to marry the king and become queen. The archbishop whispered wicked words in the king's ear, but they did not sink into his heart. The marriage still took place, and the archbishop himself had to place the crown on the bride's head. But in wicked spite, he pressed it on so tightly that it caused her pain.

A still heavier weight burdened her heart—sorrow for her brothers. She did not feel bodily pain. Her mouth was closed, a single word would cost her brothers lives. But she loved the kind, handsome king, who did more and more each day to make her happy. She loved him with all her heart, and her eyes beamed with the love she dared not speak. Oh! If she had only been able to confide in him and tell him of her grief. But she must remain silent until her great task was finished.

At night she crept into her little bedroom, which had been made to look like the cave, and wove one coat after another. But when she began the seventh, she found she had no more flax. She knew that the nettles she had to use must come from a graveyard, and that she must pluck them herself. How could she get there?

"Oh, what is the pain in my fingers compared to the torment which my heart has to bear?" she said. "I must go. I will not be denied help from heaven."

Then with a trembling heart, as if she were about to do something wicked, she crept out into the palace garden in the bright moonlight. She passed through the narrow walks and deserted streets of the city, until she reached the graveyard. She saw on one of the larger tombstones a group of ghouls. These hideous creatures took off their rags, as if they intended to bathe, and then clawing open the fresh graves with their long, skinny fingers, pulled out the dead bodies and ate the flesh! How very, very scary!

Eliza had to pass close to them, and they fixed their wicked looks on her. But she prayed silently to God, gathered the burning nettles, and carried them back to the castle.

Only one person had seen her, and that was the archbishop. He was awake while everyone else was asleep. Now he felt sure his opinion was correct. All was not right with the queen. She was a witch who had bewitched the king and all the people. Secretly he told the king what he had seen and what he feared. As the hard words came from his tongue, the carved images of the saints on the church walls shook their heads as if to say. "It is not so. Eliza is innocent." But the archbishop interpreted that a different way. He believed they witnessed against her and were shaking their heads at her wickedness.

Two large tears rolled down the king's cheeks. He went home with doubt in his heart and at night pretended to sleep. But no sleep came, for he saw Eliza get up every night and go to her cave-like room.

With each day that passed, his face became darker. Eliza saw it but did not understand why. It frightened her and made her heart tremble for her brothers. Her hot tears glittered like pearls on her rich velvet and diamonds. She was sad even though all the women who saw her wished they could be queen in her place.

She had almost finished her task. Only one coat of mail was lacking, but she had no flax left and not a single nettle. For the last time, she must go to the graveyard and pluck a few handfuls of nettles. She thought with terror of the lonely walk and of the horrible ghouls. But her will was firm, as well as her trust in God.

Eliza went, but this time the king and the archbishop followed her. They saw her vanish through the gate into the graveyard. When they came nearer, they saw the ghouls sitting on a tombstone, as Eliza had seen them. The king turned away his head, for he thought she was with them—she whose head had rested on his chest that very evening.

"The people will condemn her," he said sadly. For her supposed wickedness, she was condemned to suffer death by fire.

She was led from the palace halls to a dark cell, where the wind whistled through the iron bars. Instead of the velvet and silk dresses, they gave her the coats that she had woven for her brothers and the bundle of nettles for a pillow. But nothing they could have done would have pleased her more. She continued her painful work with joy, and prayed for God's help. Outside, the boys on the street sang jeering songs about her. Not a single person comforted her with a kind word.

Just before dark on the day before she was to be executed, she heard the flutter of swan's wings at the bars of her cell. It was her youngest brother. After a long and desperate search, he had found her. Although this would be the last night of her life, she sobbed for joy. There was still hope for her brothers if they could reach her in time. Her task was almost done.

As he had promised the king, the archbishop arrived to be with her during her last hours. But she shook her head and begged him, by looks and gestures, not to stay. For this night she knew she must finish her work, otherwise all the pain, tears and sleepless nights were in vain. The archbishop left, uttering bitter words against her. But poor Eliza knew she was innocent and diligently continued her work.

The little mice ran about the floor. They dragged the nettles to her feet to help as well as best they could. A thrush sat outside the bars of the window and sang sweetly the whole night to keep up her spirits.

It was still twilight and at least an hour before sunrise when the eleven brothers stood at the castle gate and demanded to be brought before the king. They were told that could not be for it was still night, the king slept, and they dared not disturb him.

The brothers threatened and begged. Finally, the guard appeared followed by the king himself, asking what all this noise meant. Unfortunately, at that moment the sun rose. The eleven brothers were seen no more, but eleven wild swans flew away from the castle.

All the people came pouring out the gates of the city to see the witch burned. An old horse drew the cart on which she sat. They had dressed her in a garment of coarse sackcloth. Her lovely hair hung loose on her shoulders, her cheeks were deadly pale, her lips moved silently, while her fingers still worked at the green flax. Even on her way to death, she would not give up her mission.

The ten coats lay at her feet, she was working hard on the eleventh. The mob jeered and said, "See the witch, how she mutters! She has no hymn book in her hand. She sits there with her ugly sorcery. Let us tear her coats in a thousand pieces." Then they rushed toward her and would have destroyed the coats, but at that moment eleven wild swans flew in and landed on the cart. They flapped their large wings, and the crowd drew back in alarm.

"It is a sign from heaven that she is innocent," whispered many. But they did not dare say it out loud.

As the executioner seized her by the hand to lift her out of the cart, she hastily threw the eleven coats over the swans, and they immediately became eleven handsome princes. But the youngest had a swan's wing, instead of an arm, for she had not been able to finish the last sleeve of his coat.

"Now I may speak," she cried out. "I am innocent."

Then the people, who saw what happened, bowed to her, as before a saint. But she sank lifeless in her brothers' arms, overcome with exhaustion, anguish, and pain.

"Yes, she is innocent," said the eldest brother. Then he told all that had happened. While he spoke there rose in the air a fragrance like millions of roses. Every piece of wood in the pile had taken root and thrown out branches. Now it appeared as a thick hedge, large and high, covered with roses. Above all bloomed a single white and shining flower that glittered like a star.

This flower the king plucked and placed in Eliza's bosom. Then she awoke from her swoon, with peace and happiness in her heart. All the church bells rang without anyone pulling their ropes, and birds came and circled overhead in great flocks. After that, there was a great celebration, such as no one has seen before or since. Then the king, queen and eleven brothers returned happily to the castle.

—§§§—

7. The Ugly Duckling

An ugly duckling endures rejection and hatred to make an amazing discovery. Reading time 32 minutes, 2 parts. All ages.

It was a lovely summer day in the country. The golden corn, the green oats, and the haystacks piled high in the meadows looked beautiful. The cornfields and meadows were surrounded by a large forest, in the middle of which were deep pools of water. It was a delightful day to be outside.

In a sunny spot stood a pleasant old farmhouse close to a deep river. Between the house and the water grew giant burdock plants, so high, that under the tallest of them a small child could stand up. There it was as wild as in the center of a thick forest.

In this snug and hidden retreat sat a duck on her nest, waiting for her eggs to hatch. She had grown bored waiting, for the little ones were a long time coming out of their shells, and she rarely had visitors. The other ducks preferred to swim in the river rather than climb the slippery banks to sit under a burdock leaf and gossip with her.

Finally, one shell cracked and then another. From each egg came a little bird that lifted its head and cried, "Peep, peep." "Quack, quack," said the mother. Then they all quacked as well as they could and looked about them on every side at the large green leaves. Their mother allowed them to look as much as they liked, because green is soothing to the eyes. "How large the world is," said the young ducks, when they found how much more room they had now than when they were inside an egg.

"Do you think this is the whole world?" asked the mother. "Wait until you see the garden. It stretches all the way to the pastor's field, but I have never traveled that far. Are you all out?" she asked, standing up. "No, the largest egg is still there. How long will this last? I am so tired of sitting." Then she seated herself on the one remaining egg.

"Well, how are you getting on?" asked an old duck, who was one of the few who ever paid a visit.

"One egg is not hatched yet," said the duck. "It will not break. But just look at the others. Are they not the prettiest little ducklings you have ever seen? They are the image of their father, who is so unkind that he never comes to see them."

"Let me see the egg that will not break," the old duck clucked. "I have no doubt that it's a turkey egg. I was persuaded to hatch some once. After all my care and trouble with the young ones, they were afraid of the water. I quacked and quacked, but I could not get them to go in. Let me look at the egg. Yes, that's a turkey's egg. Take my advice. Leave it where it is and teach the other children to swim."

"I think I will sit on it just a little while longer," said the duck. "I have sat so long already, a few days more will not matter."

"Please yourself," said the old duck, as she waddled away.

At last the large egg broke, and a young one crept out crying, "Peep, peep." He was large and ugly. You cannot imagine just how ugly and awkward he looked. The mother duck just stared at him and cried, "He is not at all like the others. I wonder if he really is a turkey. We'll find that out when we go to the water. He will go in, if I have to push him in myself."

The next day the weather was delightful, and the sun shone brightly on the green burdock leaves. So the mother duck took her young brood down to the water and jumped in with a splash. "Quack, quack," cried she, and one after another the little ducklings jumped in. The water closed over their heads, but they popped up in an instant and swam away with ease, their little legs paddling away underneath them. Even the ugly duckling was swimming about happily.

"Oh," said the mother, "then he must not be a turkey. Look at how well he uses his legs and how straight he holds himself in the water. He must be my own child. If you look at him properly, he is not so ugly after all. Quack, quack! Come with me now. I will take you into society, and introduce you to the other animals in the farmyard. But you must stay close to me or you will get stepped on. Above all, beware of the cat."

When they got to the farmyard, there was a lot of noise. Two families were fighting over an eel's head that, in the end, was carried off by the cat.

"See, children, that's the way of the world," said the mother duck, wiping her beak, for she had wanted the eel's head for herself. "Come now, use your legs. Show me how well you can behave. Bow your heads to that old duck over there. She is the highest born of all. She has Spanish blood, so she is rich. See that red cloth tied to her leg? That's an honor for a duck. It shows that her owner is anxious not to lose her. Come now, don't turn in your toes. A well-bred duckling spreads his feet wide apart like this. Now stretch out your neck and say "quack" like good little ducklings.

The ducklings did as they were told. But the other ducks stared, and called out, "Look, here comes another brood, as if there weren't enough of us already! What a odd-looking bird one of them is. We don't want him in *our* farmyard." Then one of them flew over and bit the ugly duckling on the neck.

"Let him alone," said the mother. "He is not doing any harm."

"Yes, but he is so big and ugly," said the spiteful duck. "He must be thrown out."

"The others are very pretty children," said the old duck, with the rag on her leg. "All but that one. I wish his mother would improve him a little."

"That is impossible, your majesty," replied the mother. "He is not pretty. But he has a very good disposition and swims as well or even better than the others. I think he will grow up pretty and perhaps be smaller. He remained too long in the egg, so his shape is not properly formed." Then she stroked his neck and smoothed his feathers, saying, "He is a drake and therefore not of so much consequence. I think he will grow up strong, though, and able to take care of himself."

"The other ducklings are graceful enough," said the old duck. "Now make yourself at home. If you find an eel's head, bring it to me."

So they made themselves comfortable. But the poor duckling, who had crept out of his shell last of all and looked so ugly, was bitten, pushed, and made fun of, not only by the ducks, but by all the other birds in the barnyard.

"He is too big," they all said. The turkey cock, who had been born into the world with spurs and fancied himself an emperor, puffed himself up like a sailboat in full sail and flew at the duckling. He became quite red in the face from anger, so much so that the poor little duckling did not know where to go. He was miserable because he was so ugly and laughed at by the whole farmyard.

That is how it went from day to day, getting worse and worse. The poor duckling was driven about by everyone. His brothers and sisters were unkind to him and said, "Ah, you ugly creature, we wish the cat would get you." Even his mother said she wished he had never been born. The ducks beat him with their wings, the chickens pecked him with their beaks, and the girl who fed the poultry kicked him with her feet. At last he could take it no more. He ran away, frightening the wild birds in the hedge as he flew over the fence.

"They are afraid of me because I am so ugly," he said. So he closed his eyes and flew until he found a large wetland where wild ducks lived. There he remained the whole night, feeling very tired and sad.

In the morning, when the wild ducks began to move about, they stared at their new companion. "What sort of a duck are you?" they all said, coming up to him.

He bowed to them and was as polite as he could be. But he did not answer their question, for he was not sure himself what kind of duck he was. "You are extremely ugly," said the wild ducks, "but that will not matter if you do not want to marry one of our family."

Poor thing! He had no thoughts of marriage. All he wanted was permission to lie among the rushes and drink water from the wetland.

After he had been there for two days, two wild geese, or rather goslings, for they had not been out of the egg for long, came and were very blunt. "Listen, friend," one said to the duckling, "you are so ugly that we like you. Will you come with us? Not far from here is another wetland where there are some pretty wild geese, all of them unmarried. Here is a chance for you to find a wife. You may even get lucky, ugly though you are."

Suddenly, "Bang, bang," sounded in the air. The two wild geese fell dead among the rushes, and the water became red with their blood. "Bang, bang," echoed far and wide, and whole flocks of wild geese flew up. The loud bangs came from every direction, for hunters had surrounded the wetland to shoot the ducks. Some had even climbed on the branches of trees. The blue smoke from the guns rose like clouds over the trees. As it floated across the water, hunting dogs ran in among the rushes, which bent beneath them wherever they went. How they terrified the poor duckling! Not knowing any better, he turned his head and hide it under his wing. At the same moment a large and fierce dog passed very near him. The dog's jaws were open, his tongue hung from his mouth, and his eyes glared terribly. He put his nose close to the duckling, showing his sharp teeth. Then, "splash, splash," he went into the water without touching the duckling.

"Oh," sighed the duckling. "I should be happy to be so ugly even a dog won't bite me."

So he lay very still, while shot after shot burst through the rushes, and gun after gun was fired over him. It was late in the day before all was quiet. Even then the poor young duckling did not dare move. He waited quietly for several hours more. Then, after looking carefully around and not daring to fly, he ran away from the wetland as fast as he could. He ran over field and meadow, through the storm and rain.

A Woman, a Cat and a Chicken

Toward evening he reached a poor little cottage that seemed ready to fall down. It only remained standing because it could not decide which way to fall. The shooting and the storm had been so violent, that the tired little duckling could go no farther. He sat down by the cottage and noticed that the door was not quite closed because one of the hinges was broken. There was a narrow opening near the bottom just large enough for him to slip through, which he did very quietly. That is how he got shelter for the night from the storm.

Now a woman, a tomcat and a hen lived in this cottage. The tomcat, which the woman called, "My little son," was her great favorite. He could arch his back and purr. He could even throw out sparks from his fur when it was stroked the wrong way. The hen had very short legs, so she was called "Chickie short legs." She laid good eggs, and her mistress loved her as if she had been her own child. In the morning when the strange visitor was discovered, the tomcat began to purr, and the hen to cluck.

"What is that noise all about?" said the old woman, looking around the room. But her sight was not very good. When she saw the duckling, she thought it was a fat duck that had strayed from home. "Oh what a prize!" she cried out. "I hope it is not a drake, for then I will have some duck's eggs. I must wait and see." So the duckling was allowed to remain on trial for three weeks, but there were no eggs. Now the tomcat was master of the house, and the hen was mistress. They always said, "We and the world," for they believed themselves to be half the world and the better half too.

The duckling thought that others might hold a different opinion on the subject, but the hen would not listen to such doubts. "Can you lay eggs?" she asked. "No. Then have the goodness to hold your tongue." "Can you raise your back, purr or throw out sparks?" said the tomcat. "No. Then you have no right to express an opinion when sensible people are speaking." So the duckling sat in a corner, feeling very low spirited, until the sunshine and the fresh air came in the room through the open door. Then he began to feel a great longing for a swim on the water, so much so that he could not help telling the hen.

"What an absurd idea," said the hen. "You have nothing else to do, so you get foolish fancies. If you could purr or lay eggs, these crazy ideas would pass away."

"But it is so much fun to swim about on the water," said the duckling. "So refreshing to feel it close over your head when you dive to the bottom."

"Fun indeed!" said the hen. "Why you must be crazy! Ask the cat. He's the cleverest animal I know. Ask him if he would like to swim in the water or dive under it, for I will not speak my own opinion. Ask our mistress, the old woman—there's no one in the world more clever than she is. Do you think she would like to swim or let the water close over her head?"

"You don't understand me," said the duckling.

"We don't understand you? Who can understand you, I wonder? Do you think you are more clever than the cat or the old woman? I will say nothing of myself. Don't imagine such nonsense, child. Thank your good fortune that you have been allowed to stay here. You are in a warm room and in a society from which you may learn something. But you are a chatterer, and your company is not very agreeable. Believe me, I speak only for your own good. I may tell you unpleasant truths. But that is a proof of my friendship. I advise you, therefore, to lay eggs and learn to purr as quickly as possible."

"I believe I must go out into the world again," said the duckling.

"Yes, do," said the hen. So the duckling left the cottage and soon found water where he could swim and dive. But because he was so ugly, all the other animals avoided him.

Autumn came, and the leaves in the forest turned to orange and gold. As winter approached, the wind caught the leaves as they fell and whirled them about in the cold air. The clouds, heavy with hail and snowflakes, hung low in the sky. The black raven cried out, "Caw, caw." If you or I had been there and seen how cold the sad little duckling was, we would have shivered with cold.

One evening, just as the sun set, a large flock of beautiful birds came out of the bushes. The duckling had never seen birds like them before. They were swans. They curved their graceful necks, and their soft plumage shown with dazzling whiteness. They uttered an unusual cry when they spread their beautiful wings to fly away from the winter cold to warmer countries across the sea. As they climbed higher and higher into the air, the ugly little duckling felt a strange sensation. He whirled himself around in the water like a wheel, stretched out his neck towards them, and uttered a cry so strange that it frightened him. How could he ever forget those beautiful, happy birds?

When at last they were out of sight, he dove under the water and rose again almost beside himself with excitement. He did not know the names of these birds, or where they had gone. But what he felt about them was different from how he had felt for any other bird he had ever seen. He was not envious of these beautiful creatures, but wished he was as lovely as they. Poor ugly creature, how glad he would have been to live with the other ducks, if they only given him a little kindness and encouragement.

The winter grew colder and colder. The ugly duckling was forced to swim about on the water to keep the opening in the ice from freezing. But every night the space in which he swam became smaller and smaller. Finally, it froze so hard that the ice in the water crackled as he moved. The duckling had to paddle with his legs as best he could to keep the space from closing up. He became exhausted at last and lay still and helpless, frozen fast into the ice.

Early in the morning a farmer who was passing by saw what had happened. He broke the ice in pieces with his wooden shoe and carried the little duckling home to his wife. The warmth revived the poor little creature.

But when the children tried to play with him, the duckling thought they wanted to hurt him like so many others. So he ran away in terror. He fluttered into the milk pan and splashed the milk about the room. Then the woman clapped her hands, which frightened him still more. He flew first into the butter, then into a tub of flour and out again. What trouble he was in now! The woman screamed and struck at him. The children laughed, yelled and tumbled over each other in their effort to catch him. But luckily he escaped out the open door. The poor duckling barely managed to get into the bushes and lie down exhausted in the newly fallen snow.

It would be very sad were I to tell you about all the misery and suffering that the poor little duckling endured during the long and hard winter. But eventually winter passed, and one morning he found himself lying in a wetland among the rushes. He felt the warm sun shining and heard a lark singing. All around him, spring was awakening nature back to life. The young bird knew his wings were strong as he flapped them against his sides and rose high in the air. They carried him on until he found himself in a large garden.

The apple trees were in full blossom, and the fragrant elders bent their long green branches down to a stream that wound around a green lawn. In the freshness of early spring, everything looked beautiful. From a thicket close by came three beautiful white swans, rustling their feathers and swimming lightly over the calm water. The duckling remembered the lovely birds from the previous fall, and felt more strangely unhappy than ever.

STORIES FOR GIRLS

"I will fly over to those royal birds," he said. "They will kill me because I am so ugly and dare to approach them. But it does not matter. Better to be killed by them than beaten by the ducks, pecked by the hens, pushed about by the girl who feeds the poultry, or starved with hunger in the winter."

Then he landed on the water and swam towards the beautiful swans. The moment they saw the stranger, they rushed to meet him with outstretched wings.

"Kill me," said the poor bird. He bent his head down to the surface of the water and waited for death.

But what did he see in the clear stream below? His own image. No longer a gray clumsy bird, ugly to look at, but a graceful and beautiful swan.

Being born from a swan's egg in a duck's nest in a farmyard had made life rough for the little bird. Now he had discovered who he really was and could escaped from all his sorrow and trouble. He could enjoy all the happiness around him. For the great swans welcomed the newcomer by swimming up to him and stroking his neck with their beaks.

Soon afterward, some little children came to the garden and threw bread and cake into the water.

"See," cried the youngest, "there is a new one." The other kids were delighted and ran to their father and mother, dancing, clapping their hands, and shouting joyously, "There is another swan here. A new one has arrived."

Then they threw more bread and cake into the water and agreed, "The new one is the most beautiful of all. He is so young and handsome." Even the old swans bowed their heads before him.

Then the once ugly duckling felt ashamed, and hid his head under his wing. He did not know what to do. He was so happy and yet not at all proud. He had been persecuted and despised for his ugliness. Now he heard the children say that he was the most beautiful of all birds.

Even the elder tree bent down its branches into the water in front of him, and the sun shone down warm and bright. Then the little duckling, now grown up into a swan, rustled his feathers, curved his slender neck, and cried happily from the depths of his heart, "I never dreamed of happiness like this while I was still an ugly duckling."

8. The Snow Queen

A brave young girl sets out on an amazing journey to rescue a friend trapped by an evil spell. Along the way, she gets help from many interesting and different people and animals.
Reading time: 1 hour, 50 minutes, 7 parts. Older children.

Story the First: A Mirror and its Broken Fragments

You must listen *very* carefully to the beginning of this story. For when we get to the end, we will know much more than we now do about a very wicked demon—one of the very worst and a real devil.

One day, when this wicked demon was feeling merry, he made a mirror which had the magical power of making everything good or beautiful that was reflected in it shrink to almost nothing. In that same mirror everything that was worthless or bad increased in size and grew powerful. In its reflection, the most beautiful landscape looked like boiled spinach. In it, people became hideous, looking as if they were standing on their heads without bodies. Their faces were so twisted that not even their closest friend would recognize them. Even one freckle on the face seemed to spread out and cover the whole of the nose and mouth. Obviously, this was a very terrible mirror.

However, the demon thought it was funny. When a good or godly thought passed through the mind of anyone, it was distorted in the glass to look like something ugly. How the demon laughed at his clever invention!

All who went to the demon's school—for he kept a school—talked about the wonderful things they saw in the mirror. They claimed that, for the very first time, people could see what the world and mankind were really like. They carried the glass about with them everywhere. At last there was no country where people had not been looked at through this distorted mirror. You may know a school where the people are just like that.

The people at this school even wanted to fly up to heaven with it to see the angels. But the higher they flew, the more slippery the glass became, until they could no longer hold on to it. It slipped from their hands, fell to the earth, and broke into millions of tiny pieces.

Broken, the mirror caused even more unhappiness. For some of the fragments were no larger than a grain of sand. They floated about the air and into every country. When one of these tiny specks flew into someone's eye, it stuck there. From that moment on, everything he saw was distorted. He could see only the worst side of everything he looked at. For the smallest sliver retained the same evil power as the whole mirror.

A few unfortunate people even got a fragment of the mirror in their hearts and that was far worse. For it made their hearts grow cold like a lump of ice. A few of the pieces were large enough that they could be used as windowpanes. It was sad to look at friends through them. Other pieces became eyeglasses and that was dreadful for those who wore them. They could see nothing either rightly or fairly. Perhaps you know people just like that.

As all this happened, the wicked demon laughed until his sides shook. It tickled him so to see all the mischief he had done. The evil that had come from his mirror, he thought, would only get worse, For there were still many little fragments of glass floating about in the air. Now you will learn what happened to two of them.

Story the Second: A Little Boy and a Little Girl

In a large town that is full of houses and people, there isn't enough room for everyone to have even the smallest of gardens. Some are forced to make do with a few flowers in flowerpots. That is unfortunate, but that's the way it has to be. It can't be helped.

In one of these large towns lived two poor children, whose parents had window gardens a little larger and better than a few flowerpots. They were not brother and sister, but they loved each other almost as much as if they had been. Their parents lived across from each other in two upstairs apartments, where the roofs of two neighboring houses projected out at each other and a gutter ran between them. In each house was a little

window, and the two windows were so close together that anyone could step across the gutter from one window to the other.

The parents of these children each had a large wooden box in which they grew kitchen herbs for their own use. There was also a small rosebush in each box, which grew splendidly. After a while the parents decided to place their two boxes on the gutter, so the boxes reached from one window to the other. Sweet peas drooped over the sides of the boxes, and the rosebushes sent out long branches, which were trained to grow around the windows and cluster together almost like an arch of leaves and flowers.

These boxes were high above the ground. The children knew they must not climb on them without permission. But they were often allowed to go out together and sit on their little stools under the rosebushes and play quietly.

In winter this fun came to an end. For the windows were frozen over and refused to open. Then the two children would warm copper pennies on the stove and hold them against the frozen windowpanes. Soon there would be a little round hole through which they could peep. The soft, bright eyes of the little boy and girl would beam through the hole in each window as they looked at each other. Then they would giggle.

The boy's name was Kay and the girl's name was Gerda. In summer they could get together by stepping from window to window. But in winter they had to go up and down long stairs and out through the snow before they could meet.

"See, there are the white bees swarming," said Kay's old grandmother one day when it was snowing.

"Have they a queen bee?" asked the little boy, for he knew that the real bees have a queen.

"To be sure they have," said the grandmother. "She is flying over there where the swarm is thickest. She is the largest of them all. She never remains on the ground, but flies up to the dark clouds. At midnight she often flies through the streets of a town and looks in windows. Then the ice freezes on the window panes into wonderful shapes that look like flowers and castles."

"I have seen that," said both the children. So they knew it must be true.

"Can the Snow Queen come in here?" asked the little girl.

"Only let her come," said the boy. "I'll put her on the stove and she'll melt." Then the grandmother smoothed the boy's hair and told him more tales.

One evening, when little Kay was at home half undressed, he climbed on a chair by the window and peeped out through the little hole in the icy window. A few flakes of snow were falling. One of them, larger than the rest, landed on the edge of one of the flower boxes. It grew larger and larger, until it became a woman, dressed in garments of white lace that looked like millions of starry snowflakes joined together. She was fair and beautiful but made of ice—shining and glittering ice. Still she was alive and her eyes sparkled like bright stars. But there was nothing peaceful in her look. She nodded towards Kay's window and waved her hand.

The little boy was frightened and jumped down from the chair. At that instant, a large bird seemed to fly by the window. The next day there was a frost and soon spring came. The sun shone, and young green leaves sprouted from the trees. The swallows built their nests and began to sit on eggs. Windows that had been frozen shut all winter were opened. The two children could now sit in the garden on the roof, high above the other rooms. How beautiful the roses were this summer! The little girl had learned a hymn in which roses were mentioned. She thought about their own roses and sang that hymn to the little boy. He sang it too:

"Roses bloom and cease to be. But we shall the Christ-child see."

Then the two children held each other by the hand and kissed the roses. They looked at the bright sunshine and spoke to it as if the Christ-child were there with them.

Those were wonderful summer days. How beautiful and fresh it seemed among rosebushes that never quit blooming. One day Kay and Gerda sat looking at a book filled with pictures of animals and birds. Just then, as the clock in the church tower struck twelve, Kay said,

"Oh, something has struck my heart!" and soon after, "There is something in my eye."

The little girl put her arm around his neck and looked at his eye, but she saw nothing.

"I think it is gone," he said. But it was not gone. It was one of those slivers from the mirror—that evil mirror of which we have spoken. It was a piece of the evil glass that made everything great and good appear small and ugly, while all that was wicked and bad became more visible and every little fault could be plainly seen. Poor Kay also had a small grain in his heart, which quickly turned it into a lump of ice.

He felt no more pain, but the glass was there working its evil. "Why do you cry?" he said at last. "It makes you look ugly. There is nothing the matter with me now. Oh, see!" he cried suddenly. "That rose is worm-eaten, and this one is quite crooked. After all they are ugly roses, just like the box in which they stand." Then he kicked the boxes with his foot and pulled off the two roses.

"Kay, what are you doing?" cried the little girl. When he saw how frightened she had become, he tore off another rose. Then he jumped through his own window to get away from little Gerda.

After that, when she brought out the picture book, he said that, "It was only fit for babies in long clothes." When his grandmother told stories, he would interrupt her with "but." When he could manage it, he would get behind her chair, put on a pair of spectacles, and imitate her very cleverly, just to make people laugh.

By-and-by he began to mimic the speech and walk of people he saw on the street. All that was peculiar or disagreeable in a person he would imitate. People said, "That boy is clever. He has a remarkable genius." But there was nothing special about him. It was the piece of glass in his eye and the coldness in his heart that made him act like that.

He would even tease little Gerda, who loved him with all her heart. His games became very different. They were no longer the sort that children play. When it was snowing one winter day, he brought out a magnifying glass. He held out the tail of his blue coat and let the snowflakes fall on it.

"Look in this glass, Gerda," said he. She saw how every flake of snow was magnified and looked like a beautiful flower or a glittering star. "Isn't that clever?" said Kay, "and much more interesting than looking at real flowers. There is not a single fault in them. The snow-flakes are perfect until they begin to melt." You and I can see that Kay was beginning to prefer cold, mechanical perfection to the warmth and richness of life.

Soon after that, Kay appeared in large thick gloves with his snow sled on his back. He called up the stairs to Gerda, "I've got to go to the great square where the other boys play and ride." Away he went.

In the great square, the boldest of the boys would tie their sleds to the country people's carts and ride behind them out of town. This was great fun.

But while they were amusing themselves and Kay with them, a great sled came by. It was painted white and in it sat someone wrapped in a rough white fur and wearing a white cap. The sled drove twice around the square. Kay fastened his own little sled to it, so that when it went away, he was pulled behind. It went faster through the next street. Then the person who drove it turned around and nodded pleasantly to Kay, as if they had already met one another. But whenever Kay tried to loosen his little sled from the great sled, the driver turned around and nodded again. So Kay sat still as they drove quickly out the town gate.

Then the snow began to fall so heavily that the little boy could not see an arm's length in front of him. Still they drove on. Kay tried to loosen the cord, so the large sled would go on without him. But it was no use. His little sled held fast and away they went like the wind. He called out loudly, but no one heard him, while the snow beat on him, and the sled flew on. Every now and then the giant sled gave a jump as if it were going over hedges and ditches. The boy was frightened, and tried to say a prayer, but he all he could remember was the multiplication table.

The snowflakes became larger and larger, until they looked like large white chickens. Then, all at once, they sprang up on one side of the sled like soldiers standing at attention, and the great sled stopped. The person who was driving it stood up. The fur and the cap were made entirely of snow and fell off. Kay saw a lady, tall and white. It was the Snow Queen that he had seen the winter before.

"We have gone a great distance," said she. "But why do you tremble? Here, crawl into my warm fur coat." Then she seated him beside her in the sled. As she wrapped the fur around him, he felt like he was sinking into a deep snowdrift.

"Are you still cold," she asked, as she kissed him on the forehead. The kiss was colder than ice. It went through to his heart, which was already almost a lump of ice. He felt as if he were going to die, but only for a moment. He soon seemed quite well and did not notice the cold around him.

"My sled! Don't forget my sled," was his first thought. Then he looked and saw that it was tied fast to one of the white chickens, which flew behind them with the sled at its back. The Snow Queen kissed little Kay again, and by this time he had forgotten about little Gerda, his grandmother, and everyone at home.

"Now you must have no more kisses," she said, "or I will kiss you to death."

Kay looked at her and saw that she was beautiful. He could not imagine a more lovely and intelligent face. She did not seem to be made of ice, as she had when he had seen her through his window and she had nodded to him. In his eyes she was perfect, and he did not feel the least bit afraid. He told her he could do mental arithmetic as far as fractions, and that he knew the number of square miles and the number of inhabitants in the country.

She always smiled in a way that made him think that he did not know enough yet. She looked around the vast sky as she flew higher and higher with him on a black cloud, while the storm blew and howled as if it were singing old songs. They flew over woods and lakes, over sea and land. Below them roared the wild wind. The wolves howled and the snow crackled. Over them flew black screaming crows and above all shone the moon, clear and bright. That was how Kay passed through that long winter's night. By daylight he was sleeping at the feet of the Snow Queen.

Story the Third: The Flower Garden of the Woman Who Could Do Magic

How was little Gerda after Kay disappeared? No one knew what had become of him. Nor could anyone give the slightest information, except some boys who said that he had tied his little sled to a large sled that had driven down the street and out the town gate. No one knew where he had gone. Many tears were shed for him, and little Gerda wept bitterly for a long time. She said she knew he must be dead, that he had drown in the river which flowed close by the school. Those long winter days were very dreary. But at last spring came, bringing warm sunshine. "Kay is dead and gone," said little Gerda to herself.

"I don't believe it," said the sunshine.

"He is dead and gone," she said to the sparrows.

"We don't believe it," they replied. At last little Gerda began to doubt it herself. "I will put on my new red shoes," she said one morning, "the ones Kay has never seen. Then I'll go down to the river and ask for him."

It was quite early when she kissed goodbye to her grandmother, who was still asleep. She put on her red shoes and went all alone out the town gate to the river. "Is it true that you have taken my little friend away from me?" said she to the river. "I will give you my red shoes if you will give him back to me."

It seemed as if the waves nodded to her strangely. So she took off her red shoes, which she liked better than anything else in the world, and threw them into the river. But they fell near the bank, and the waves soon brought them back to shore. It seemed that the river would not take from her what she loved best, because it could not give her Kay back.

But she thought the shoes had not been thrown out far enough. So she crept into a boat that lay among the reeds, climbed to its farthest end and again threw the shoes into the water. Unfortunately, the boat was not fastened to the shore, and her movement sent it gliding out into the river. When she saw this, she scrambled to reach the other end of the boat. But before she could do that, it was more than a yard from the shore and drifting away faster than ever.

Little Gerda was frightened, for she could not swim. She began to cry, but no one heard her except the sparrows, and they could not carry her to land. They flew along the shore and sang, as if to comfort her, "Here we are! Here we are!"

The boat floated with the stream. Little Gerda sat quite still with only stockings on her feet. The red shoes floated after her, but she could not reach them because the boat stayed ahead of them. As bad as her situation was, the banks on each side of the river were certainly pretty.
There were beautiful flowers, old trees, and sloping fields in which cows and sheep were grazing. But there was not a single person who could help her.

Perhaps the river wants to carry me to little Kay, thought Gerda. Then she became more cheerful, raised up her head, and looked at the beautiful green banks. So the boat floated on for many, many hours.

Eventually, she came to a large cherry orchard, in the middle of which stood a small red house with red, blue and yellow windows. It had a thatched roof. On the outside were two wooden soldiers, who saluted her as she sailed past. Gerda called out to them, for she thought they were alive, but of course they did not answer. As the boat drifted nearer to shore, she saw what they really were.

Then Gerda called still louder. Out of the house came a old woman, leaning on a crutch. She wore a large hat to shade her from the sun. On that hat were painted all sorts of pretty flowers.

"You poor little child," said the old woman. "How did you manage to come all this distance on such a fast moving river?"

The old woman walked into the water, seized the boat with her crutch, drew it to land, and lifted Gerda out. Gerda was glad to be on dry ground, although she was afraid of the strange woman.

"Come and tell me who you are," said she, "and how you came here."

Gerda told her everything, while the old woman shook her head, and said, "Hum-hum." When Gerda finished her story, she asked the old woman if she had seen little Kay. The old woman told her he had not passed by that way, but he likely would come by someday. So she told Gerda not to be sorrowful, but to taste the cherries and look at her flowers. They were far better than any picture book, for each could tell a story.

Then she took Gerda by the hand and led her into the little house, closing the door after her. The windows were very high. Since the panes were red, blue, and yellow, the daylight shone through them in all sorts of wonderful colors. On the table were delicious cherries, and Gerda got permission to eat as many as she wanted. While she was eating, the old woman combed her long flaxen hair with a golden comb, and the glossy curls hung down on each side of her round and pleasant face, which looked as fresh as a rose in bloom.

"I have been wishing for a dear little girl like you for a long time," said the old woman. "Now you must stay with me and see how happy we will be together."

While she went on combing little Gerda's hair, Gerda thought less and less about her adopted brother Kay, for the old woman could conjure, although she was not a wicked witch. She conjured only a little for her own amusement, and, in this case, because she wanted to keep Gerda.

The old woman went into her garden and stretched out her crutch toward all the rosebushes, beautiful though they were. They immediately sank into the dark ground, so no one could tell where they had once been. The old woman was afraid that if little Gerda saw roses she would think of those at home, remember little Kay, and run away.

Then she took Gerda into the flower garden. How fragrant and beautiful it was! Every flower imaginable for every season of the year was there in full bloom. No picture book could have had more beautiful colors. Gerda jumped for joy and played until the sun went down behind the tall cherry trees. Then she slept in an elegant bed with red silk pillows embroidered with colored violets. She dreamed like a princess on her wedding day.

The next day and for many days afterward, Gerda played with the flowers in the warm sunshine. She knew every one of the many flowers, and yet it seemed as if one kind of flower was missing. But what it was, she could not say. Then one day, as she sat looking at the old woman's hat and the painted flowers on it, she saw that the prettiest of them all was a rose. The old woman had forgotten to take it off her hat when she made all the roses sink into the earth. After all, it is difficult to keep your thoughts together in everything. One little mistake can upset even the most clever arrangements.

"What, are there no roses here?" cried Gerda. She ran into the garden and examined all the beds. She searched and searched for roses. There was not one to be found. Then she sat down and wept. Her tears fell on the very place where one of the rosebushes was. Her warm tears moistened the earth, and the rosebush sprouted up at once, blooming as it had when it had sank. Gerda embraced it and kissed the roses. She thought of the beautiful roses at home and, with them, of little Kay.

"Oh, how I have been held back!" said the little girl. "I must look for little Kay. Do you know where he is?" she asked the roses. "Do you think he's dead?"

All the roses answered, "No, he is not dead. We have been in the ground where all the dead lie. Kay is not there."

"Thank you," said little Gerda. Then she went to the other flowers, looked into their little cups, and asked, "Do you know where my little Kay is?"

But each flower, as it stood in the sunshine, dreamed only its own little fairy tale of history. Not one knew anything of Kay. Gerda heard many stories from the flowers, as she asked them one after another about him.

What did the tiger lily say? "Hark, do you hear the drum? 'Turn, turn.' There are only two notes, always, 'turn, turn.' Listen to the women's song of mourning! Hear the cry of the priest! In her long red robe, the Hindu widow stands by the funeral pile. The flames rise around her as she places herself on the dead body of her husband. But the Hindu woman is thinking of the living one in that circle and of her son, who lit those flames. Those shining eyes trouble her heart more painfully than the flames that will soon consume her body to ashes. Can the fire of the heart be extinguished in the flames of the funeral pile?"

"I don't understand that at all," said little Gerda.

"That is my story," said the tiger lily.

What says the morning glory? "Near a narrow road stands an old knight's castle. Thick ivy creeps over the old ruined walls, leaf over leaf, even to the balcony, on which stands a beautiful maiden. She leans out and looks up the road. No rose on its stem is fresher than she. No apple blossom, blown by the wind, floats more lightly than she moves. Her rich silk rustles as she bends over and cries out, 'Will he come?'

"Is it Kay you mean?" asked Gerda.

"I am only speaking of a story in my dream," answered the flower.

What said the little snowdrop? "Between two trees a rope is hanging. There is a piece of board on it. It is a swing. Two pretty little girls, in dresses white as snow and with long green ribbons fluttering from their hats, are sitting on it, swinging. Their brother who is taller than they, stands in the swing. He has one arm around the rope to steady himself. In one hand he holds a little bowl and in the other a clay pipe. He is blowing bubbles. As the swing goes back and forth, the bubbles fly upward, showing the most beautiful changing colors. The last bubble hangs from the bowl of the pipe and sways in the wind. On goes the swing. Then a little black dog comes running up. He is almost as light as the bubble. He raises himself on his hind legs and wants to ride the swing. But it does not stop and the dog falls. Then he barks and gets angry. The children stoop toward him and the bubble bursts. A swinging plank, a light sparkling picture—that is my story."

"It may be all very pretty what you are telling me," said little Gerda. "You speak so mournfully and yet you do not mention little Kay at all."

What do the hyacinths say? "There were three beautiful sisters, fair and delicate. The dress of one was red, of the second blue, and of the third pure white. Hand in hand they danced in the bright moonlight by a calm lake. But they were human beings not fairy elves. A sweet fragrance attracted them, and they disappeared into the forest. Here the fragrance was stronger. Three coffins, in which lay the three beautiful maidens, glided out of the thickest part of the forest and across the lake. The fireflies flew lightly over them, like little floating torches. Are the dancing maidens sleeping or are they dead? The scent of the flower says they are dead. The evening bell tolls their last song."

"You make me sad," said little Gerda. "Your perfume is so strong, that you make me think of the dead maidens. Ah! Is little Kay really dead then? The roses have been in the earth, and they say no."

"Cling, clang," tolled the hyacinth bells. "We are not tolling for little Kay. We do not know him. We sing our song, the only one we know."

Then Gerda went to the buttercups that were glittering among the bright green leaves.

"You are little bright suns," said Gerda. "Tell me if you know where I can find my friend."

The buttercups sparkled gaily and looked again at Gerda. What song could the buttercups sing? It was not about Kay.

"The bright warm sun shone on a little court on the first warm day of spring. His bright beams rested on the white walls of the neighboring house. Close by bloomed the first yellow flower of the season, glittering like gold in the sun's warm ray. An old woman sat in her arm chair at the door. Her granddaughter, a poor and pretty servant maid, came to see her for a short visit. When she kissed her grandmother there was gold everywhere—the gold of the heart in that holy kiss. It was a golden morning. There was gold in the beaming sunlight, gold in the leaves of the lowly flower, and on the lips of the maiden. There, that is my story," said the buttercup.

"My poor old grandmother!" sighed Gerda. "She is longing to see me and grieving for me as she did for little Kay. But I shall soon go home and take Kay with me. It is no use asking the flowers. They know only their own songs and can give me no answers."

Then she tucked up her dress, so she could run faster. But the narcissus caught her by the leg as she jumped over it. So she stopped, looked at the tall yellow flower, and said, "Perhaps you know something."

Then she stooped down quite close to the flower and listened. What did he say?

"I can see myself, I can see myself," said the narcissus. "Oh, how sweet is my perfume! Up in a little room with a bow window, stands a little dancing girl, half undressed. She stands sometimes on one leg, and sometimes on both, and looks as if she would place the whole world under her feet. She is nothing but a delusion. She is pouring water out of a teapot on something which she holds in her hand. It is her dress sash. 'Cleanliness is a good thing,' she says. Her white dress hangs on a peg. It has also been washed in the teapot and dried on the roof. She puts it on and ties a saffron-colored handkerchief around her neck, which makes the dress look whiter. See how she stretches out her legs, as if she were a flower showing off on a stem. I can see myself, I can see myself."

"What do I care for all that," said Gerda. "You should not tell me such silly stuff."

Then Gerda ran to the other end of the garden. The door was fastened, but she pressed against the rusty latch, and it gave way. The door sprang open, and little Gerda ran out with bare feet into the wide world. She looked back three times, but no one seemed to be following her. At last she could run no longer, so she sat down to rest on a large stone. When she looked around, she saw that the summer was over, and autumn far advanced. She had known nothing of this in the beautiful garden, where the sun shone and the flowers grew all year round.

"Oh, how I have wasted my time?" said little Gerda. "It is already autumn. I must not rest any longer." She stood up to go on. But her bare feet were cut and sore. Everything around her looked cold and bleak. The long willow leaves were yellow. The dew drops fell like water. Leaf after leaf dropped from the trees. Only the sloe-thorn still bore fruit, but the sloes were sour and set her teeth on edge. How dark and weary the whole world had become!

Story the Fourth: The Prince and Princess

Growing tired, Gerda was forced to rest. Just opposite where she sat, she saw a large black crow hopping across the snow toward her. He stood looking at her for some time. Then he shock his head and said, "Caw, caw. Good day, good day." He pronounced the words as plainly as he could because he meant to be kind to the little girl. Then he asked her where she was going all alone in the wide world.

The word "alone" Gerda understood very well and knew how much it said. So she told the crow the whole story of her life and adventures and asked him if he had seen little Kay.

The crow nodded his head very gravely and said, "Perhaps I have— it may be."

"Really! Do you think you have?" cried little Gerda. She kissed the crow and hugged him almost to death with joy.

"Gently, gently," said the crow. "I believe I know. I think it may be little Kay. But he has certainly forgotten you by this time for a princess."

"Does he live with a princess?" asked Gerda.

"Yes, listen," replied the crow. "But it is so difficult to speak your language. If you understand the crow language, I can explain it better. Do you?"

"No, I have never learned it," said Gerda. "My grandmother understands it and used to speak it to me. I wish I had learned it."

"It does not matter," answered the crow. "I will explain as well as I can, although it will be badly done." He told her what he had heard. "In this kingdom where we now are," said he, "there lives a princess, who is so wonderfully clever that she has read all the newspapers in the world and forgotten them too, although she is so clever. A short time ago, as she was sitting on her throne, which people say is not such an agreeable seat as is often supposed, she began to sing a song which starts with these words:

'Why should I not be married?'

'Why not indeed?' said she. So she determined to marry if she could find a husband who knew what to say when he was spoken to—not just one who could look grand, for that was tiresome. She called together all her court ladies with the beat of a drum. When they heard her plans, they were pleased. 'We are so glad to hear it,' said they. 'We were talking about it ourselves the other day.' You may believe that every word I tell you is true," said the crow. "For I have a tame sweetheart who goes freely about the palace, and she told me all this."

Of course his sweetheart was a crow, for 'birds of a feather flock together.' One crow always picks another crow.

"Newspapers were published immediately, with a border of hearts, and the initials of the princess among them. They gave notice that every young man who was handsome was free to visit the castle and speak with the princess. Those who could respond properly when spoken to, were to make themselves at home at the palace. The one who spoke best would become her husband. Yes, yes, you may believe me, it is all as true as I sit here," said the crow. "The young men came in crowds. There was a great deal of crushing and running about, but no one succeeded on the first or second day. They could all speak very well when they were outside in the streets. But when they entered the palace gates and saw the guards in silver uniforms, the footmen in their golden uniforms on the staircase, and the great halls lighted up, they became terribly confused.

When they stood before the throne on which the princess sat, they could do no better than repeat the last words she had said. She had no wish to hear her own words over and over. It was as if they had all taken something to make them sleepy while they were in the palace, for they did not recover or speak until they were back again in the street. There was quite a long line of them reaching from the town gate to the palace. I went myself to see them," said the crow. "They were hungry and thirsty, for at the palace they did not get even a glass of water. Some of the wisest had taken a few slices of bread and butter with them, but they would not share it with their neighbors. They believed that if others went to the princess looking hungry, their chances would be better."

"But Kay! Tell me about little Kay!" said Gerda. "Was he among the crowd?"

"Wait a bit, we are just coming to him. On the third day, there came marching cheerfully to the palace a little guy, without horse or carriage, his eyes sparkling like yours. He had beautiful long hair, but his clothes were very poor."

"That was Kay!" said Gerda joyfully. "Oh, then I have found him." She clapped her hands.

"He had a little knapsack on his back," added the crow.

"No, it must have been his sled," said Gerda. "For he went away with it."

"It may have been so," said the crow. "I did not look at it very closely. But I know from my tame sweetheart that he passed through the palace gates, saw the guards in their silver uniforms and the servants in their golden uniforms on the stairs. But he was not in the least embarrassed. 'It must be very tiring to stand on these stairs,' he said. 'I prefer to go in.' The rooms were blazing with light. Councilors and ambassadors walked about on bare feet, carrying golden vessels. It was enough to make anyone feel serious. His boots creaked loudly as he walked, and yet he was not at all uneasy."

"It must be Kay," said Gerda. "I know he had new boots on. I heard them creak in grandmother's room."

"They really did creak," said the crow. "Yet he went boldly up to the princess herself, who was sitting on a pearl as large as a spinning wheel. All the ladies of the court were present with their maids and all the knights with their servants. Each of the maids had another maid to wait on her. The knights' servants had their own servants, as well as a page each. They all stood in circles around the princess. The nearer they stood to the door, the prouder they looked. The servants' pages, who always wore slippers, could hardly be looked at, they held themselves up so proudly by the door."

"It must be quite awful," said little Gerda. "But did Kay win the princess?"

"If I had not been a crow," said he. "I would have married her myself, although I am engaged. He spoke just as well as I do, when I speak the crow language, so I heard from my tame sweetheart. He was quite relaxed and pleasant. He said he had not come to woo the princess, but to hear her wisdom. He was as pleased with her as she was with him."

"Oh, certainly that was Kay," said Gerda. "He is so clever. He can work mental arithmetic and fractions. Will you take me to the palace?"

"It is very easy to ask that," replied the crow. "But how are we to manage it? However, I will speak to my sweetheart and ask her advice. For I must tell you it will be very difficult to gain permission for a little girl like you to enter the palace."

"Oh yes. But I shall get permission easily," said Gerda. "For when Kay hears I am here, he will come quickly and fetch me."

"Wait for me here by the picket fence," said the crow, shaking his head as he flew away.

It was late in the evening before the crow returned. "Caw, caw," he said, "she sends you greeting and here is a little roll that she took from the kitchen for you. There is plenty of bread there, and she thought you might be hungry. It isn't possible for you to enter the palace by the front entrance. The guards in silver uniform and the servants in gold uniforms would not allow it. But do not cry. We will manage to get you in. My sweetheart knows a back staircase that leads to the royal bedrooms. She knows where to find the key."

Then they went down a great avenue which ran through the royal garden. The leaves were falling one after another, and they could see the lights in the palace being put out. The crow led little Gerda to the back door, which stood ajar. Oh, how little Gerda's heart beat with fear and longing. It was as if she were going to do something wrong. Yet she only wanted to know where little Kay was. "It must be he," she thought, "with those clear eyes and that long hair." She could fancy she saw him smiling at her, as he used to at home when they sat among the roses. He would certainly be glad to see her, to hear what a long distance she had come for his sake, and to know how sorry they were at home because he had not come back. Oh, what joy and fear she felt! They were now on the stairs. In a small closet at the top, a lamp was burning. In the middle of the floor stood the tame crow, turning her head from side to side and gazing at Gerda, who curtseyed as her grandmother had taught her to do.

"My betrothed has spoken highly of you, my little lady," said the tame crow. "Your life history, *Vita*, as it is called in Latin, is very touching. If you will take the lamp, I will walk before you. We will go straight along this way, then we will meet no one."

"It seems like some one is behind us," said Gerda, as something rushed by her like a shadow on the wall. Then horses with flying manes and thin legs, hunters, ladies and gentlemen on horseback, glided by her, like shadows on the wall.

"They are only dreams," said the crow, "they are coming to fetch the thoughts of the great people out hunting."

"All the better, for we can pass by their beds more safely. I hope that when you rise to honor and favor, you will show a grateful heart."

"You may be quite sure of that," said the crow from the forest.

They now came into the first hall, the walls of which were hung with rose-colored satin and embroidered with artificial flowers. Here the dreams again flitted by them, but so quickly that Gerda could not tell what they were. Each hall appeared more splendid than the last. It was enough to bewilder anyone.

After some time, they reached a bedroom. The ceiling was like a great palm tree with glass leaves of the most costly crystal. In the center were two beds, each resembling a lily hung from a stem of gold. One, in which the princess lay, was white, while the other was red. In this Gerda went to look for little Kay. She pushed one of the red leaves aside and saw a brown neck. Oh, that must be Kay! She called his name out quite loud and held the lamp over him. The dreams rushed back into the room on horseback. He woke and turned his head around. It was *not* little Kay! The prince was only like him in the neck. Still he was young and handsome. Then the princess peeped out of her white bed and asked what was the matter. Little Gerda wept and told her story, and all that the crows had done to help her.

"You poor child," said the prince and princess. Then they praised the crows and said they were not angry at what they had done, but that it must not happen again. This time they would be rewarded.

"Would you like to have your freedom?" asked the princess, "or would you prefer to be raised to the position of court crows, with all that is left in the kitchen for yourselves?"

Both the crows bowed and begged to have a fixed appointment, for they thought of their old age and said it would feel good to have provided for their old days, as they called it. Then the prince got out of his bed and gave it up to Gerda—he could do no more. She lay down, folded her little hands, and thought, "How good everyone is to me, men and animals too." Then she closed her eyes and fell into a sweet sleep. All the dreams came flying back again to her. They looked like angels, and one of them drew a little sled, on which sat Kay, and he nodded to her. But all that was only a dream and vanished as soon as she awoke.

The following day Gerda was dressed from head to foot in silk and velvet. The prince and princess invited her to stay at the palace for a few days and enjoy herself. But she begged for a pair of boots along with a small carriage and a horse to draw it, so she might go into the world and look for Kay. She got not only boots but also a muff, so she was dressed perfectly for the cold. When she was ready to go, at the door she found a coach made of pure gold, with the coat-of-arms of the prince and princess shining on it like a star. The coachman, footman and outriders were all wearing golden crowns on their heads.

The prince and princess themselves helped her into the coach, and wished her success. The forest crow, who was now married, accompanied her for the first three miles. He sat by Gerda's side, as he could not bear riding backwards. The tame crow stood in the doorway flapping her wings. She could not go with them, because she had been suffering from a headache ever since the new appointment, no doubt from eating too much. The coach was filled with sweet cakes and under the seat were fruit and gingerbread nuts. "Farewell, farewell," cried the prince and princess. Gerda and the crow wept. Then after a few miles, the crow also said "Farewell." That was the saddest parting of all. He flew to a tree and stood flapping his black wings as long as he could see the coach, which glittered in the bright sunshine.

Story the Fifth: Little Robber-Girl

The golden coach drove on through a thick forest, where its gold lighted the way like a torch and dazzled the eyes of some robbers, who could not bear to let it pass by unrobbed.

"It's gold! It's gold!" cried they, rushing forward and seizing the horses. Then they struck the jockeys, the coachman, and the footman dead, and pulled little Gerda out of the carriage.

"She is well-fed and pretty. She has eaten lots of nuts," screeched the old robber woman, who had a long beard and eyebrows that hung down over her eyes. "She will taste as good as a little lamb. How delicious she will be when we eat her!" As she said that, she brought out a sharp knife that glittered horribly. "Oh!" screamed the old woman the same moment. Her daughter had bitten her on the ear and was holding her back. The daughter was a wild and naughty girl, and the mother called her an ugly thing. Angry at her daughter, she forgot to kill Gerda.

"She will play with me," said the little robber girl. "She will give me her muff and her pretty dress. She will sleep with me in my bed." Then she bit her mother again, making her spring in the air and jump about. All the robbers laughed and said, "See how she dances with her young cub." "I will ride in the coach," said the little robber girl. She wanted to have her own way in everything. She was very strong-willed and stubborn.

She and Gerda seated themselves in the coach, and it drove away, over stumps and stones, into the depths of the forest. The little robber girl was about the same size as Gerda, but much stronger. She had broader shoulders and darker skin. Her eyes were quite black, and she had a sad and mournful look. She clasped little Gerda around the waist and said in what she thought was kindness, "They won't kill you as long as you don't make us mad at you. I suppose you are a princess."

"No," said Gerda. Then she told her story, and how much she cared for Kay.

The robber girl looked earnestly at her, nodded her head slightly, and said, "They won't kill you, even if we do get angry with you. For I will do it myself." Then she wiped Gerda's eyes and stuck her hands in the beautiful muff which was so soft and warm.

The coach stopped in the courtyard of a robber's castle, the walls of which were cracked from top to bottom. Ravens and crows flew in and out of the holes and crevices, while two giant bulldogs, either of which looked as if it could swallow a man, were jumping about but weren't allowed to bark. In the large and smoky hall a bright fire was burning on the stone floor. There was no chimney, so the smoke went up to the ceiling and found a way out for itself. Soup was boiling in a large pot, while hares and rabbits were roasting on the spit over a fire.

They had something to eat and drink. Then the robber girl said, "You will sleep with me and all my animals tonight." She took Gerda to a corner of the hall, where some straw and carpets were laid down. Above them, on planks and perches, were more than a hundred pigeons, who all seemed asleep, although they moved slightly when the two little girls came near.

"All these pigeons belong to me," said the robber girl. She seized the one nearest to her, held it by the feet, and shook it until it flapped its wings. "Kiss it," cried she, flapping it in Gerda's face.

"There are the wood pigeons," she continued, pointing to some boards and a cage that had been mounted on the walls near one of the openings. "The rascals would fly away, if they were not locked up. And here is my old sweetheart Ba." She hauled out a reindeer by the horn. He wore a bright copper ring around his neck and was tied up. "We are obliged to keep him tied up, or he would run away. I tickle his neck every evening with my sharp knife, which frightens him very much." Then the robber girl drew out a long knife from a chink in the wall and let it slide gently over the reindeer's neck. The poor animal began to kick. Then the little robber girl laughed and pulled Gerda into bed with her.

"Will you have that knife with you while you are asleep?" asked Gerda, looking at it in great fright.

"I always sleep with the knife," said the robber girl. "No one knows what may happen. But tell me again all about little Kay, and why you went out into the world."

Gerda repeated her story again, while the wood pigeons in the cage over her cooed, and the other pigeons slept. The little robber girl put one arm across Gerda's neck and held the knife in the other. Soon she was fast asleep and snoring. But Gerda could not close her eyes at all. She did not know if she would live or die. The robbers sat around the fire, singing and drinking, and the old woman stumbled about. It was a terrible sight for a little girl to see.

Then the wood pigeons said, "Coo, coo. We have seen your little Kay. A snow chicken carried his sled while he sat in the carriage of the Snow Queen. They drove through the wood while we were lying in our nest as little pigeons. She blew on us, and all the young ones died except us two. Coo, coo."

"What are you saying up there?" cried Gerda. "Where was the Snow Queen going? Do you know anything about it?"

"She was most likely traveling to Lapland, where there is always snow and ice. Ask the reindeer that is fastened with a rope."

"Yes, there is always snow and ice there," said the reindeer. "It is a wonderful place to live. You can leap and run about freely on the sparkling ice plains. The Snow Queen has her summer home there, but her largest castle is near the North Pole on an island called Spitzbergen."

"Oh, Kay, little Kay!" sighed Gerda.

"Lie still," said the robber girl, waking up, "or I will stick my knife in you."

In the morning Gerda told the little robber girl everything that the wood pigeons had said. The robber girl looked quite serious, nodded her head, and said, "That is talk, that is all talk. Still it is something. Do you know where Lapland is?" she asked the reindeer.

"Who would know better than I?" said the animal, with his eyes sparkling. "I was born and brought up there. Before I was captured, I used to run about its snow-covered plains."

"Now listen," said the robber girl. "All our men have gone away. Only mother is here, and here she will stay. But at noon she always drinks out of a big bottle, and afterwards she sleeps for a little while. When that happens, I'll do something for you. For now, just wait." She jumped out of bed, clasped her mother around the neck, and pulled her by the beard, crying, "My own little nanny goat, good morning." Then her mother pulled on the robber girl's nose until it was bright red. Yet they did it all for love.

When the mother had drunk from the bottle and gone to sleep, the little robber girl went to the reindeer and said, "I should like very much to tickle your neck a few times more with my knife because it makes you look so funny. But never mind. I will untie your cord, and set you free, so you can run back to Lapland. But you must make good use of your legs and carry this little maiden to the castle of the Snow Queen, where her friend is. You have heard what she told me, for she spoke loud enough, and you were listening."

Then the reindeer jumped for joy. The little robber girl lifted Gerda on his back and had the good sense to tie her on. She even gave Gerda her own cushion to sit on.

"Here are your fur boots back," she said. "For it will be very cold up there. But I must keep the muff. It's so pretty. However, you will not freeze for the lack of it. Here are my mother's large warm mittens. They will reach to your elbows. Let me put them on. There, now your hands look just like my mother's."

Gerda wept for joy.

"I don't like to see you upset," said the little robber girl. "You ought to feel very happy now. Here are two loaves and a ham, so you won't starve." These she fastened to the reindeer. Then the little robber girl opened the door and coaxed in the giant dogs. She cut the rope with which the reindeer was held and said, "Now run, but be sure to take good care of the little girl."

Gerda waved a hand with the great mitten on it to the robber girl and called back, "Thank you very much. Good bye." Away flew the reindeer, over stumps and stones, through a great forest filled with trees, over marshes and plains, as quickly as he could. The wolves howled, and the ravens screeched. Above them, the sky quivered with red lights like flames of fire. "Those are my friends, the old northern lights," said the reindeer. "See how they flash." He ran on day and night, faster and faster. But the loaves and the ham were eaten by the time they reached Lapland.

Story the Sixth: The Lapland Woman and the Finland Woman

They stopped at a poor-looking little hut. The roof sloped nearly to the ground, and the door was so low that the family who lived there had to creep in and out on their hands and knees. There was no one at home but an old Lapland woman, who was cooking fish by the light of an oil lamp. The reindeer told her Gerda's story, after having first told his own, which seemed to him the more important. But Gerda was so cold that she could not speak. "Oh, you poor things," said the Lapland woman, "you have a long way to go yet. You must travel more than a hundred miles farther to Finland. The Snow Queen lives there now, and she burns blue lamps every evening. I will write a few words on a dried fish, for I have no paper. You can take it from me to the Finland woman who lives there. She can give you better information than I."

So when Gerda was warmed and had something to eat and drink, the woman wrote a few words on the dried fish, and told Gerda to take great care of it. Then she tied her again on the reindeer, and he set off at full speed. Flash, flash, went the beautiful blue northern lights in the sky the whole night long.

After some time, they reached Finland and knocked at the chimney of the Finland woman's hut, for it had no door above the ground. They crept in, but it was so terribly hot inside that woman wore scarcely any clothes. She was small and dirty looking. She loosened little Gerda's dress and took off the fur boots and mittens, so Gerda could bear the heat. Then she placed a piece of ice on the reindeer's head and read what was written on the dried fish. After she read it three times, she knew it by heart. She popped the fish into the soup saucepan, as she knew it was good to eat. She never wasted anything.

The reindeer told his own story first, then little Gerda's. The Finland woman's bright eyes twinkled, but she said nothing. "You are so clever," said the reindeer. "I know you can tie all the winds of the world with a piece of twine. If a sailor unties one knot, he has a fair wind. When he unties the second, it blows hard. But if the third and fourth are loosened, then there comes a storm that will uproot entire forests. Can't you give this little maiden something powerful which will make her as strong as twelve men, so she can overcome the Snow Queen?"

"The power of twelve men!" said the Finland woman, "that would be of little use against the Snow Queen." But she went to a shelf, took down and unrolled a large skin, on which were written many wonderful letters. She read until the perspiration ran down from her forehead. But the reindeer begged so hard for little Gerda, and Gerda looked at the Finland woman with such pleading and tearful eyes, that the woman's own eyes began to twinkle. She drew the reindeer into a corner, and whispered to him while she laid a fresh piece of ice on his head.

"Little Kay really is with the Snow Queen," she told them, "but he finds everything there so much to his taste and liking that he believes it is the finest place in the world. But this is because he has a piece of broken glass in his heart and a little piece of glass in his eye. These must be taken out, or he will never be human again, and the Snow Queen will keep her power over him."

"But can you give little Gerda something to help her to defeat this terrible power?"

"I can give her no greater power than she already has," said the woman. "Don't you see how strong that is? How men and animals have wanted to serve her. Look how well she has gotten through the world, barefooted and poor. She cannot receive any power from me greater what she now has with her purity and innocence of heart. If she cannot get to the Snow Queen's palace herself and remove the glass fragments from little Kay, we can do nothing to help her. Two miles from here the Snow Queen's garden begins. You can carry the little girl that far. Set her down by the large bush covered with red berries which stands in the snow. Do not stay gossiping, but come back here as quickly as you can." Then the Finland woman lifted little Gerda on the reindeer, and he ran away with her as quickly as he could.

"Oh, I have forgotten my boots and my mittens," cried little Gerda, as soon as she felt the cutting cold, but the reindeer dared not stop. He ran on until he reached the bush with the red berries. Here he set Gerda down and kissed her, the great bright tears trickling down the animal's cheeks. Then he left her and ran back as fast as he could.

There stood poor Gerda, without shoes, without gloves, in the middle of dreary, ice-cold Finland. She ran forward as quickly as she could, with a whole regiment of snowflakes fluttering around her. They did not fall from the sky, which was quite clear and glittering from the northern lights. The snowflakes ran along the ground. The nearer they came to her, the larger they appeared. Gerda remembered how large and beautiful they looked through a magnifying glass. But these were really larger and more terrible. For they were alive and were the guards of the Snow Queen. They had the strangest shapes. Some were like great porcupines, others like twisted serpents with their heads stretching out, and some few were like little fat bears with their hair bristled up. But all were dazzlingly white, and all were living snowflakes.

Then little Gerda repeated the Lord's Prayer. The cold was so great that she could see her own breath coming out of her mouth like steam as she uttered the words. As she continued her prayer, the steam seemed to increase until it took the shape of little angels, who grew larger the moment they touched the ground. They all wore helmets on their heads and carried spears and shields. Their number increased more and more. By the time Gerda had finished her prayer, a whole army of angels stood around her. They thrust their spears into the terrible snowflakes and shattered them into a hundred pieces. Now little Gerda could go on with courage and safety. The angels rubbed her hands and feet, so she felt the cold less. Then she hurried on to the Snow Queen's castle.

Story the Seventh: The Palace of the Snow Queen

Now we must see what Kay is doing. Sadly, he was not thinking of little Gerda and never imagined that she might be standing in the front of the palace where he was.

The walls of the Snow Queen's palace were made of drifted snow, and its windows and doors were made from the cold and biting winds. There were more than a hundred rooms in it, all made as if they had been built of snow blown together. The largest of them extended for several miles. They were all lit by the northern lights in the sky. They were so large and empty, so icy cold and glittering! There was nothing fun to do in them, not even dancing bears to watch. For with the storm as music, the bears could have danced on their hind legs and shown their good manners. There were no games of snapdragon or touch or even gossip over the tea table for the young lady foxes. Empty, vast and cold were the frozen halls of the Snow Queen. The flickering flame of the northern lights could be plainly seen from every part of the castle, whether they rose high or low in the sky. In the middle of its empty, endless hall of snow was an icy lake, broken on its surface into a thousand strange shapes. Each piece resembled another much like works of art do. In the center of this lake the Snow Queen sat when she was at home. She called her frozen lake "The Mirror of Reason." She said it was the best, and indeed, the only one of its kind in the world.

Little Kay was quite blue with cold, indeed almost black, but he did not feel it. For the Snow Queen had kissed away the icy shivering, and his heart was a lump of ice. He spent his time dragging some sharp, flat pieces of ice to and fro, placing them together in different positions. It was as if he wanted to make something out of them, just as we try to make pictures with those little tablets of wood we call a Chinese puzzle. Kay's fingers were very artistic. It was the icy game of reason that he played, and in his eyes the figures were very remarkable and of the highest importance. This opinion was a result of the piece of glass sticking in his eye. He composed many complete figures, forming different words. But there was one word he had never managed to form, although he wished very much to do so. It was the word "Eternity." The Snow Queen had said to him, "When you find out that, you will be your own master, and I will give you the whole world and a new pair of skates." But he was not able to do it, even though he tried as hard as he could.

"Now I must hurry away to warmer countries," said the Snow Queen. "I will look into the black craters at the tops of the burning mountains, Etna and Vesuvius they are called. I will make them white with snow. That will be good for them and, when the snow melts, for the lemons and grapes in the fields below." Away flew the Snow Queen, leaving little Kay all alone in the emptiness of the great hall, which was many miles long. He sat and looked at his pieces of ice. He was thinking so deeply and sat so still, that anyone might have thought he was frozen.

At just this moment little Gerda came through the great door of the castle. Cold, cutting winds were raging around her, but she said a prayer and the winds sank down as if going to sleep. She went on until she came to the large empty hall and caught sight of Kay. She recognized him, ran quickly up to him, and threw her arms around his neck. She held him tightly and said, "Kay, dear little Kay, I have found you at last."

But he sat quite still, stiff and cold.

Then little Gerda wept hot tears, which fell on his chest and penetrated to his heart. They thawed the lump of ice and washed away the little piece of glass that had stuck there. He looked at her and she sang:

> Roses bloom and cease to be. But we shall the Christ-child see.

Kay burst into tears. He wept so much that the splinter of glass floated from his eye. He recognized Gerda, and said, joyfully, "Gerda, dear little Gerda, where have you been all this time, and where have I been?" He looked all around and said, "How cold it is and how large, lifeless, and empty it looks." He clung tightly to Gerda, and she laughed and wept for joy.

It was so wonderful to see them reunited that even the pieces of ice danced about. When they were tired and went to lie down, they formed themselves into the letters of the word that the Snow Queen had said he must find out before he could be his own master and have the whole world and a new pair of skates. Then Gerda kissed his cheeks, and they turned red and warm.

She kissed his eyes, and they shone like her own. She kissed his hands and his feet, and he became quite healthy and cheerful. The Snow Queen might come home now if she pleased, for there stood his freedom, in the very word she had demanded, written in shining letters of ice.

They took each other by the hand and walked side by side out of the great palace of ice. They talked about his grandmother and about the roses on the roof. As they walked, the winds were at rest, and the sun shown brightly. When they arrived at the bush with red berries, there stood the reindeer waiting for them. He had brought another young reindeer whose udders were full. The children drank her warm milk and kissed her. Then the two reindeer carried Kay and Gerda to the Finland woman, where they warmed themselves thoroughly in the hot room. She gave them directions for their journey home. Next, they went to the Lapland woman, who made some new clothes for them and put their sleighs in order. Both reindeers ran by their side and followed them as far as the border of the country, where the first green leaves were already budding. After everyone had said good bye, Kay and Gerda sadly left the two reindeer and the Lapland woman.

As they travelled, the birds sang and the forest was full of green young leaves. Then out of it came a beautiful horse, which Gerda remembered as one that had drawn the golden coach. A young girl rode on it with a shining red cap on her head and pistols in her belt. It was the little robber girl, who had grown tired of staying at home. She was going first to the north country. If that did not suit her, she planned to try other parts of the world, until she found a place she liked. She knew Gerda and Gerda remembered her. It was a happy meeting.

"You must be very special to travel this far from home," the robber girl said to Kay. "I would like to know if you deserve for someone to go to the end of the world to rescue you."

But Gerda patted the robber girl's cheeks and asked about the prince and princess.

"They have gone on a trip to foreign countries," said the robber girl.

"And the crow?" asked Gerda.

"Oh, the crow is dead," she replied. "His tame sweetheart is now a widow and wears a bit of black wool around her leg. She mourns pitifully. But tell me how you managed to get your friend back."

Then Gerda and Kay told her what had happened.

"Snip, snap, snare! It's all right at last," said the robber girl happily.

Then she took both their hands and promised that if she ever passed through the town where the two lived, she would give them a visit. Then she rode out into the wide world.

Gerda and Kay went hand-in-hand toward home. As they traveled, spring appeared more lovely that it ever had before. Soon they recognized the large town where they lived and the tall steeples of the churches in which the sweet bells were ringing a merry peal as they entered.

They found their way to his grandmother's door. The two went upstairs to the little room where everything looked just as it had been when they left. The old clock was going "tick, tick," and the hands pointed to the time of day. But as they passed through the door into the room, they realized that they had both grown up and become a man and a woman. The roses on the roof were in full bloom and peeped in the window. There stood the little chairs on which they had sat when they were children. Kay and Gerda sat down, each on their own chair, and held each other by the hand. As they did, the cold and empty grandeur of the Snow Queen's palace vanished from their memories like a painful dream.

The grandmother sat in God's bright sunshine and read aloud to them from the Bible, "Except you become as little children, you can in no way enter into the kingdom of God." Kay and Gerda looked into each other's eyes, and all at once understood the words of the old song,

Roses bloom and cease to be. But we shall the Christ-child see.

And they both sat there, grown up, yet children at heart, and it was summer—a warm, beautiful summer.

—§§§—

9. The Little Match Girl

The saddest imaginable story with surprisingly happy ending.
Reading time: 10 minutes. All ages.

It was terribly cold and quickly growing dark on the last evening of the old year. The snow was coming down fast and covering everything in a thick white blanket. In the cold and dark, a poor little girl, with a bare head and naked feet, roamed the streets all alone.

She had been wearing a pair of slippers when she left home that morning. But they were of little use. They were too large, so large, in fact, that they belonged to her mother. The little girl had lost them running across a street to avoid two horse-drawn carriages that were racing along very fast and might have crushed her beneath their steel-covered wheels. Afterward, she could not find one of the slippers. A boy grabbed the other and ran away, saying that he would use it as a cradle when he had children of his own.

So the little girl went on in her naked feet, which soon turned red and blue from the cold. In an old apron that was much too big for her, she carried some matches. She had a bundle of them in her hands and had tried very hard that day to sell them to strangers on the street. But no one had bought a single match the whole day. No one had even given her a penny out of kindness. Shivering with cold and hunger, she crept along, ignored by all and unseen by most. The snowflakes fell on her long hair, which hung in curls down to her shoulders. Poor little child, she looked so miserable and so lonely.

It was New Year's Eve, and the holiday rush had left people too busy to notice this sad and shy little girl. Lights were shining from every window, and there was a smell of roast goose in the air. Yes, she remembered that, although it meant little to her. There would be no delicious meal waiting for her when she got home, no warm, brightly lit dining room.

In a corner between two houses, she sat down on the hard, frozen ground and huddled up as best she could to protect herself from the cold wind that bit through her thin, tattered clothes. She drew her bare feet tightly beneath her, but that did little to make her warm. She did not dare go home, for she had sold no matches that day and did not have even a single penny. For that her father would beat her. Besides, it was almost as cold there as here. For they were poor and had only a thin roof to protect them. The wind howled through that, even though the largest holes had been stuffed with straw and rags.

Her little hands were now almost frozen from the cold. Ah! Perhaps a burning match would warm them! If she could just take one from the bundle and strike it against the wall. One small match to warm her fingers, that was all.

She drew it out. "Scratch!" How it sputtered as it burned! It gave a warm, bright light, just like a candle, as she held her hand over it. How wonderfully bright and warm! The little girl felt like she was sitting in front of a large iron stove with polished brass feet and a bright brass ornament on top. How it glowed! In her mind it seemed so delightfully warm that she stretched out her feet to warm them. Then the match went out, the stove vanished, and she had only the terrible cold and a half-burnt match in her hand.

Quickly, she scratched another match against the wall. It burst into flame. Where its light fell, the wall became as transparent as a veil. She could see into the room behind. The table was covered with a snowy white tablecloth on which stood a delicious dinner and a steaming roast goose, stuffed with apples and dried plums. Then something amazing happened! The goose jumped down from the table and waddled across the floor, with a knife and fork in its breast, all the way up to the little girl. Then the match went out, everything went dark, and nothing remained but the damp, cold wall in front of her.

STORIES FOR GIRLS

Without wasting a moment, she lit another match and found herself seated under a beautiful Christmas tree. It was even larger and more beautifully decorated than the one she had seen through a glass door at a rich merchant's home. Thousands of candles were burning in its green branches. Colored pictures, like those she had seen in store windows, looked down from the walls. The little girl stretched out her hand toward them. Then the match went out.

The Christmas lights she had seen rose higher and higher until they seemed like the stars in the sky. Then she saw a star fall, leaving behind a bright streak of fire. "Someone is dying," thought the little girl. For her old grandmother—the only one who had ever loved her and who was now dead—had told her that when a star falls, a soul was going to be with God.

She rubbed another match on the wall, and its light shone all around her. In its brightness stood her grandmother, clear and shining, kind and loving. "Grandmother," cried the little girl, "Take me to be with you. Otherwise, I know you will disappear when the match burns out. You will vanish just like the warm stove, the roast goose, and the bright Christmas tree." Then she made haste to light the whole bundle of matches, for she wanted to keep her grandmother with her always.

Burning together, the bundle of matches glowed with a light that was brighter than the noonday sun. In their light, her grandmother had never appeared so loving or so beautiful. She took the little girl in her arms, and both flew up in brightness and joy to a place far above the earth, to a place where there was neither cold nor hunger nor pain, for they were with God.

As the next morning dawned, some people who were out early discovered the poor little match girl, with pale cheeks and a smiling mouth, leaning against the wall. She had frozen to death on the last evening of the year. Now the New Year's sun shone on her cold and lifeless body. The child still sat, in the stillness and stiffness of death, holding matches in her hand, one bundle of which had burnt almost to her fingers.

"She tried to warm herself before she died," said some. No one imagined the beautiful things she had seen, nor the wonder and glory she had entered into with her grandmother on that New Year's Day.

10. Five Peas in One Pod

Five peas grow up in one pod, almost exactly alike. But only one lives in a way that makes the world a happier place.
Reading time: 12 minutes. All ages.

There were once five peas in one pea pod. They were green and the pod was green, so they believed that the whole world must be green too. That was a very natural conclusion.

The pod grew, and the peas grew. They adjusted themselves to their position inside and sat all in a row. The sun shone outside and warmed the pod and the rain made it transparent. Inside, it was bright in the day and dark at night. As they sat there, the peas grew bigger and more thoughtful. They asked questions about the meaning of life and felt there must be something they were supposed to do with their lives.

"Will we stay here *forever*?" asked one. "Won't we grow hard sitting so long? There must be something outside the pod. I am sure of that."

As weeks passed, the peas became yellow, and the pod became yellow. "All the world is turning yellow, I suppose," said they. Perhaps they were right.

Suddenly they felt a pull on the pod. It was torn off, held in human hands, and then slipped into the pocket of a jacket along with some other full pods.

"Soon we will be opened," said one, which was just what they all wanted. Then they would be able to see the bigger world outside.

"I would like to know which of us will travel the furthest," said the smallest of the five. "We will soon see."

"What will happen will happen," said the largest pea.

"Crack" went the pod as it burst, and the five peas rolled out into the bright sunshine. There they lay in a child's hand. A little boy was holding them tightly. He said they would make fine peas for his pea-shooter. He put one in and shot it.

"Now I am flying out into the wide world," said that pea. "Catch me if you can," and he was gone in a moment.

"I," said the second, "intend to fly straight to the sun. It shines the brightest, so it must the most important. That will suit me exactly." Away he went.

"We will settle down and take it easy wherever we find ourselves," said the next two. "But before that we must roll about and travel." They certainly did fall on the floor and roll about before they got into the pea-shooter. But they were put in anyway. "We will go farther than the others," they cried.

"What will happen will happen," said the last, as he was shot out of the pea-shooter. As he spoke, he flew up against an old board under an apartment window and fell into a little crevice, which was almost filled with moss and soft earth. The moss closed itself around him, and there he lay, a captive indeed, but *not* unnoticed by God.

"What will happen will happen," he said to himself.

Within that little upstairs apartment lived a poor woman, who went out to clean stoves, chop wood into small pieces, and perform all sorts of hard work, for she was strong and industrious. Yet she always remained poor. At home in the apartment lay her only daughter, not quite grown up and very delicate and weak. For a whole year she had been forced to stay in bed. It seemed she could neither live nor die.

"She is going to be with her little sister," said the woman sadly. "I had but the two children, and it has not been easy to support both of them. But the good God helped me in my work and took one of them to Himself, so He could care for her. Now I would gladly keep my other daughter. But I suppose they are not to be separated, and my sick girl will soon go to be with her sister above." But the sick girl remained where she was. Quietly and patiently she lay all day long, while her mother was away at work.

Spring came and early one morning the sun shone brightly through the little window and threw its rays on the floor of the room. Just as the mother was going to work, the sick girl looked at the lowest pane of the window. "Mother," she called out, "what can that little green thing be that peeps in at the window? It's moving in the wind."

The mother stepped to the window and half opened it. "Oh!" she said surprised, "there is a little pea which has taken root and is putting out its green leaves. How could it have got into this crack? Well, here is a little garden for you to amuse yourself with." So the bed of the sick girl was placed near the window, so she might see the budding plant. Then her mother went to work.

"Mother, I believe I will get well," said the sick child in the evening. "The sun has shone in here so brightly and warmly today, and the little pea is thriving so well. I will get better too and go out into the warm sunshine again."

"God grant it!" said the mother, though she did not believe it would be so. But she used a little stick to prop up the green plant that had given her child such pleasant hopes of life, so it would not be broken by the winds. She tied a piece of string to the windowsill and to the upper part of the window frame, so the pea's tendrils might twine around it as it grew. And it did shoot up. It almost seemed to grow from day to day.

"Now a flower is coming," said the old woman one morning. At last she began to encourage the hope that her sick daughter might really get well. She saw that her daughter was speaking more cheerfully and during the last few days had raised herself in bed in the morning to look with sparkling eyes at her little garden that had only a single pea plant. A week afterward, the girl sat up for a whole hour for the first time, feeling very happy by the open window in the warm sunshine. Outside the little plant grew stronger, and on it there was a pink pea blossom in full bloom. The little maiden bent down and gently kissed the delicate leaves. For her, this day was a celebration of life.

"Our heavenly Father Himself has planted that pea and made it grow and flourish to bring joy to you and hope to me, my blessed child," said the happy mother. She smiled at the flower, as if it had been an angel from God.

But what became of the other peas? The one who flew out into the wide world and said, "Catch me if you can," fell into a gutter on the roof of a house and ended his travels in the crop of a pigeon. The two lazy ones were carried just as far, for they also were eaten by pigeons, so they were at least of some use. But the fourth, who wanted to reach the sun, fell into a sink and lay there in the dirty water for days and weeks, until he swelled to a great size.

"I am getting beautifully fat," said the pea. "I expect I shall burst at last. No pea could do more than that I think. I am the most remarkable of all the five peas that were in the shell." And the sink confirmed the opinion. "I," said the sink, "think my pea is the best."

But the young girl stood at the open apartment window, with sparkling eyes and the rosy hue of health on her cheeks. She folded her thin, pale hands over the pea blossom and thanked God for what He had done.

—§§§—

11. There's No
Doubt About It

*A hen plucks just one feather, but the account of that grows to
something amazing as the story spreads from bird to bird.
Reading time: 8 minutes. All ages.*

It was a terrible thing to happen!" said a hen in a part of the town
where *it* had not taken place. "It was the most terrible thing that could
happen in a hen roost. I cannot sleep alone tonight. It is good that so
many of us sit in the roost together." Then she told a story that made
the feathers on the other hens bristle up, and the rooster's comb fall
down. There was no doubt about it. No doubt at all.

But we will begin at the beginning, and the beginning is to be found
in a hen roost in another part of the town. The sun was setting, and the
chickens were flying back to their roost. One hen, with white feathers
and short legs, always laid her eggs according to the rules and
regulations. As a hen, she was completely respectable in every way.
Then it happened. As she was flying to her roost, she plucked herself
with her beak and a tiny feather came out. That was all, nothing more.

"There it goes," she said. "The more I pluck, the more beautiful I
become." She said this merrily, for she was a good-natured and
sensible hen, and, moreover, as has been said, she was very respectable
and easy to get along with. With that she settled down in the roost and
went to sleep.

It was dark all around, and hen sat close to hen. But the one who sat nearest to her merry neighbor did not sleep. She had heard and yet not heard, as we often have to do in this world in order to live in peace. But she could not keep it from her neighbor on the other side. "Did you hear what was said? I mention no hen's names. No, I will not. But there is a hen here in the roost who intends to pluck herself featherless in order to look pretty. If I were a rooster, I would despise her for that."

Just over these chickens sat an owl nest, with a father owl, a mother owl, and some little owls. The family has sharp ears and heard every word their neighbor below had said. They rolled their eyes, and the mother owl, beating her wings, said: "Don't listen to her! Can you believe that? I heard it with my own ears, and one has to hear a great deal before they fall off. One of the chickens has so forgotten what is proper to a hen that she plucks out all her feathers to attract a rooster."

"Prenez garde aux enfants!" said father owl in French to express his great shock. "Children should not hear such things."

"But I must tell our neighbor owl. She is such a wise owl." With that the mother owl flew away.

"Too-whoo! Too-whoo!" They both hooted into their neighbor's dovecot to the doves who were roosting inside. "Have you heard? Have you heard? Too-whoo! There is a hen who has plucked out all her feathers for the sake of the rooster. She will freeze to death, if she is not frozen already. Too-whoo!"

"Where? Where?" cooed the doves.

"In the neighbor's yard. I have as good as seen it myself. It is almost unbecoming to tell the story. But there is no doubt about it."

"Believe every word of what we tell you," said the doves as they cooed down into the poultry yard. "There is a hen—no, some say that there are two—who have plucked out all their feather to attract the attention of the rooster. It is a dangerous game, for one can easily catch cold and die from fever, and both of them are dead already."

"Wake up! Wake up!" crowed the rooster and flew on to his board. Sleep was still in his eyes, but yet he crowed out: "Three hens have died of their unfortunate love for a rooster. They had plucked out all their feathers. It is a horrible story: I will not keep it to myself, but let it go farther as a warning."

"Let it go farther," shrieked the bats, and the hens clucked and the cocks crowed, "Let it go farther! Let it go farther!" In this way the story travelled from poultry yard to poultry yard. At last it came back to the place where it had started.

"Five hens," it now ran, "have plucked out all their feathers to show which of them had grown leanest for love of the rooster. Then they all pecked at each other until the blood ran down, and they fell down dead, to the shame of their family and the great loss of their owner."

The hen who had lost the loose little feather naturally did not recognize her own story and, being a respectable hen, said: "I despise those fowls, but there are more of that kind around. Such things ought not to be concealed, and I will do my best to get the story into the papers, so that it becomes known throughout the land. These hens richly deserve what happened to them and their family too."

So it got into the papers, it was printed. and there is no doubt about it. The same could happen to us. If we are not careful, one plucked feather can easily grow into five featherless and dead hens.

12. The Girl Who Stepped on a Loaf of Bread

*A self-centered, proud and cruel girl learns through hardship
to be kind and generous. Reading time: 20 minutes. All ages.*

There was once a girl who stepped on a loaf of bread to keep from getting her shoes muddy. Though her story is well-known, perhaps you have not yet heard of the terrible things that happened to her because of that one tiny deed.

Her name was Inge. Her family was poor, but that did not keep her from being proud, self-centered and cruel. When she was still a little girl, she thought it great fun to catch flies, tear off their wings, and force them to crawl about. When she grew older, she would take beetles and stick pins through them. Then she would place a little scrap of paper near their feet. The poor beetles would seize it and turn it over and over in their struggle to get free of the pin. Seeing that, she would laugh and say, "The beetle is reading. See how he turns the paper over." As she grew older, she grew worse rather than better. Most unfortunate of all, she was pretty. As a result, she was often excused when she should have been punished.

"Your stubborn will needs to be controlled," her mother often told her. "As a little child you would trample on my apron. One day I fear you will trample on my heart." Sadly, her mother's fear came true.

Perhaps because she was so pretty, Inge was sent to the home of some rich people who lived many miles from her village. They were kind and treated her as their own child. Unfortunately, they dressed her so well that her pride became even worse. After she had been there for a year, the mistress of the house said to her, "Inge, you ought to go home and see your parents."

So Inge left to visit her home. But she really only wanted to show herself off in her home village, letting people would see how well-dressed she had become. When she reached the entrance to the village, she saw the young men and women her age talking with each other. She also saw her own mother with them, resting on a stone with a bundle of sticks lying in front of her. When she saw her mother, Inge turned around and left the village. She was now so nicely dressed that she felt ashamed of her mother, a poorly clad woman who lived by picking up wood in the forest. No, Inge did not turn back from pity for her mother's poverty. She turned back because she was afraid of what the other young people might think of her.

Another six months went by and her mistress said, "You really ought to go home and visit your parents, Inge. I will give you a large loaf of bread to take to them. I am sure they will be glad to see you."

So Inge put on her best clothes and a new pair of shoes. She set out for home, walking very carefully, so her new shoes stayed neat and clean. Of course, there is nothing wrong with that. But when she got to where the path led across a marsh, she came to a mud puddle. Now you will *not* believe what she did next! She threw the loaf into the mud and stepped on it, so she could get across the puddle without getting her new shoes dirty. As she stood with one foot on the loaf and the other lifted up to step forward, the strangest thing happened. The loaf began to sink under her. Lower and lower it sank, until she disappeared into the ground. Soon, only a few bubbles on the surface of the puddle pointed to where she had gone.

But where did Inge go? She sank down to the brewery of the Marsh Woman that some say is related to elves. We all know about elves from stories we have heard and pictures we have seen. But we know little about the Marsh Woman herself, except that a mist rises from the meadows in the summer because she is brewing something deep underground.

The Marsh Woman's brewery is so terrible, that no one wants to stay there. In fact, a pile of mud is a king's palace compared to it. As Inge sank down, her arms and legs trembled and became as cold and stiff as marble. Her foot had stuck to the loaf and it pulled her down like a golden ear of corn bends a corn stalk.

Soon, an evil spirit took charge of Inge, and carried her to an even worse place. There she saw many unhappy people waiting in misery for the gates of mercy to be opened for them. It would take too long to describe the terrible things these people suffered. Inge's punishment consisted of standing like a statue, with her foot stuck to the loaf. She could move her eyes and see the misery around her, but she could not turn her head. When she saw people looking at her, she thought they were admiring her pretty face and fine clothes, for she was still vain and proud. She had forgotten how dirty her clothes had become in the Marsh Woman's brewery. A snake had fastened itself to her hair and hung down her back, From each fold in her dress a great toad peeped out and croaked like a sick poodle. Worst of all was the terrible hunger that tormented her because she could not stoop down and break off a piece of the bread on which she stood. Her back was too stiff, and her whole body was like stone. Flies without wings crawled all over her face and eyes. She winked and blinked, but they could not fly away, for their wings had been pulled off. This, added to the hunger she felt, was a horrible torture.

"If this lasts much longer," she said, "I will not be able to bear it." But it did last, and she did have to bear it without being able to help herself.

A warm tear, soon followed by many others, fell on her head, rolled down her face and neck, and dropped on to the loaf of bread. Who was weeping for Inge? She had a mother in the world still, and the tears of sorrow that a mother sheds for her child will always find their way to her child's heart. But they often increase the torment instead of bringing relief. Inge could hear all that was said about her in the world she had left. Everyone seemed cruel to her. The sin she had committed by stepping on the loaf was well known. A man herding cows on a nearby hill has seen it.

Her mother wept, "Ah, Inge! What grief you have caused me." Then Inge would tell herself, "Oh, I wish that I had never been born! My mother's tears are no good now. I can't change."

Then the words of the kind people who had adopted her came to her ears saying, "Inge was a sinful girl, who did not value the gifts that God gave her and instead trampled them under her feet."

"Ah," thought Inge, "they should have punished me and driven my selfish attitude out of me."

Inge even became famous in a bad sort of way. A song was made up about, "The girl who stepped on a loaf to keep her shoes from becoming dirty," and for a time everyone sang it. The story of her sin was taught to the little children as a lesson. They called her "Wicked Inge" and said she was naughty and ought to be punished. Inge heard all this, and that made her heart still more hard and bitter.

Then one day, while hunger and grief were gnawing at her thin body, she heard a little, innocent child who had been listening to the story of the vain, haughty Inge, burst into tears and cry, "But will she never return to our world again?"

The little girl heard the sad reply, "No, she will never come up again."

"But if she were to say she was truly sorry, ask for pardon, and promise never to do it again?" asked the little one.

"Yes, then she might come up, but she will never ask for pardon," was the answer.

"I wish she would," said the child, who was sad when she heard the story, "then she could come back to our world. I would be happy to give up my doll and all my toys for her. Poor Inge! Her life is so sad."

These kind words penetrated to Inge's inmost heart and seemed to do her good. It was the first time ever someone had said, "Poor Inge!" without saying something about her faults. A little innocent child was weeping and praying for mercy for her. It made her feel strange. She would gladly have cried herself, so it added to her torment to find she could not weep. As she suffered in a place where nothing seemed to change, years passed on earth. Inge heard her name less frequently. But one day a sigh reached her ear with the words, "Inge! Inge! What a grief you have been to me! I said it would be so." Those were the last words of her dying mother.

Not long after that, Inge heard her aged mistress say, "Ah, poor Inge! Will I ever see you again? Perhaps I may, for we do not know what will happen in the future." But Inge knew that her kind mistress would never come to the dreadful place where she was.

Then a long time passed when nothing was said about Inge—not one single thing good or bad. People, it seemed, had forgotten about her. Then she heard her name pronounced once more and saw what seemed to be two bright stars shining above her. They were two gentle eyes closing in death. Many years had passed since the little girl had wept about "poor Inge." That girl was now an old woman whom God was taking to Himself.

In our last hour of existence, the events of our whole life often appear before us. In that hour the old woman remembered how, as a child, she had shed tears over the story of Inge. With her dying breath, she prayed for her now. As the eyes of the old woman closed on earth, the eyes of her soul opened on the hidden things of eternity. Then she, in whose last thoughts Inge had been so vividly present, saw how deeply the poor girl had sank. She burst into tears. In heaven, as she had done as a little child on earth, she wept and prayed for poor Inge. Her tears and her prayers echoed through that dark and empty space that surrounded the poor, tormented, and captive Inge. Then through her tears an unexpected mercy came to Inge.

In her mind, Inge seemed to repeat over and over again every sin she had committed on earth. She trembled, and tears she had never been able to weep before came to her eyes. Still, it seemed impossible that the gates of mercy would open for her. But while she thought of that in deep sorrow, a beam of radiant light shot through the darkness around her. More powerful than the sunbeam that dissolves a snowman children have built and more quickly than a snowflake melts on the warm lips of a child, the cold and stony body of Inge was changed.

As a little bird she soared, as fast as lightning, up to our world. She had become a timid and shy bird. She seemed to shrink with shame when she meet any living creature and hurriedly concealed herself in the dark corner of an old ruined wall. There she sat cowering, unable to make a sound.

Yet how quickly the little bird discovered what she had never noticed before, the beauty of everything around her. The sweet, fresh air, the soft radiance of the moon as its light spread over the earth, the fragrance that came from bush and tree, made her happy as she sat there clothed in her new, bright plumage. All creation spoke of God's kindness and love. The bird tried to express the thoughts that stirred in her heart, just as the cuckoo and the nightingale do in the spring, but she could not. Yet heaven can be heard in a song of praise, even from a worm, and the notes trembling in the breast of the bird were as audible to Heaven as the Psalms of David were before they fashioned themselves into words and song.

Christmas came, and a farmer who lived near the old wall stuck up a pole with some ears of corn fastened to the top, so the birds might feast and rejoice in the happy, blessed time. On Christmas morning the sun rose and shone on those ears of corn, which were soon surrounded by twittering birds. Then, from a hole in the wall came the singing of the bird as she came from her hiding place to perform her first good deed on earth. In heaven it was well known who this bird really was.

The winter was very cold. The ponds were covered with ice, and there was little food for beasts of the field or birds of the air. Our little bird flew along the highway. Here and there she found, in the ruts of the road, a grain of corn, or in other places some crumbs. Of these she ate only a few. But she called around her the other birds, so they might eat. She flew into the towns and looked about. Wherever a kind hand had placed bread on a windowsill for the birds, she only ate a single crumb for herself and gave all the rest to other birds. That winter she collected so many crumbs and gave them to other birds, that they equalled the weight of the loaf on which Inge had stepped to keep her shoes clean. When the last bread crumb had been found and given away, the her gray wings became white and spread themselves out for flight.

"Look at that beautiful seagull!" cried the children, when they saw her as she dived into the sea and rose again into the clear sunlight, white and glittering. No one could tell where she went then. But some claimed she flew straight into heaven.

13. The Jewel of Wisdom

To help their father discover the truth about eternal life, four brothers journey far from home. They are rescued by their blind sister and through her the secret of life is discovered. Reading time: 50 minutes, 5 parts. Older children.

Far, far to the east in India, which seemed in those days the world's end, stood the Tree of the Sun—a noble tree, such as you and I have never seen and perhaps may never see.

The branches of this enormous tree spread out for miles around like an entire forest, with each of its smaller branches forming a complete tree. Palms, beeches, pines, plane trees, and many other kinds of trees, which are found in all parts of the world, were small branches shooting out from that one great tree. The larger branches, with their knots and curves, formed valleys and hills, clothed with velvety green and covered with flowers.

Everywhere you looked, there was a beautiful meadow or a lovely garden. Birds from the four corners of the world came here. Birds from the forests of America, from the rose gardens of Damascus, and from the deserts of Africa, where the elephant and the lion boast of being the only rulers. Birds from cold regions flew here, and the stork and swallow too. But the birds were not the only living creatures there. Deer, squirrels, antelopes, and hundreds of other beautiful, light-footed animals called it home.

At the summit of the tree was a large garden. On a hill in the middle of that garden stood a castle of crystal glass with a view in every direction. Each tower on that castle was like a lily flower. Within the stem was a winding staircase through which you could climb to the top and step out on the leaves much as you would step on a balcony. At the center of the flower was a glittering, circular hall, above which no roof stood other than the sky with its sun and stars.

Just as much beauty, but of another kind, appeared below in the wide halls of the castle. On the walls were moving pictures of the world, with scenes showing what was happening, so there was no need to read the newspapers. In fact there were no newspapers in the place. All that was news was there to be seen in living pictures by those who wished it.

But all that knowledge would have been too much for even the wisest man in the world. And, in fact, the wisest man did live there. His name is very difficult to say. You or I would not be able to pronounce it, so it may be omitted from this story. He knew everything that a man on earth can know or imagine. Every invention already in existence or yet to be was known to him and much, much more.

But still everything on this earth has its limit. The wise king Solomon was not half as wise as this man. He could govern the powers of nature and ruled over powerful spirits. Even Death itself was obliged to come every morning and give him a list of those who were to die during the day.

Yet even wise King Solomon had to die at last. That fact often filled the thoughts of the great man in the castle. He knew that, however high he might soar above other men in wisdom, he too would some day die. Even sadder, he knew that his children would fade away like the leaves of the forest and become dust. In his mind's eye he saw the entire human race wither and fall like leaves from a tree. He saw new men fill their places, but the leaves that fell never sprouted again. They crumbled to dust or were absorbed into other plants.

"What happens to man," asked the wise man of himself, "when touched by the angel of death? What can death be? The body decays and the soul. Yes, what is the soul, and where does it go?"

"To eternal life," says the comforting voice of religion.

"But what is this change? Where and how will we exist after death?"

"Above, in heaven," answers the pious man. "It is there where we hope to go."

"Above!" repeated the wise man, fixing his eyes on the moon and stars above him. He saw that for our earth above and below were constantly changing places, and that the position varied according to the spot on which a man found himself. He also knew that even if he climbed to the top of the highest mountain, the air, which to us seems clear and transparent, would there be dark and cloudy. The sun would have a coppery glow and send forth no rays, and our earth would lie beneath him wrapped in an orange-colored mist. How narrow are the limits to human sight. How little can be seen by the eye of the soul. How very little do the wisest among us know of that which is so important for us all.

In the most secret chamber of his castle lay the greatest treasure on earth—the Book of Truth. The wise man had read it through page after page. Every man may read in this book, but only in fragments. To many eyes the characters seem so mixed and confused that the words cannot be read. On some pages the writing is often so pale or so blurred that the page appears blank. The wiser a man becomes, the more he can read. Those who are wisest read most.

This wise man knew how to join sunlight and moonlight with the light of reason and the hidden powers of nature. Through this stronger light, many things in the book's pages became clear to him. But in the part of the book entitled "Life after Death," he could not see a single word clearly. That bothered him very much. Here on earth, would he never be able to obtain a light that would show everything written in the Book of Truth?

Like the wise King Solomon, he understood the language of animals and could translate their talk into song. But that gave him no answer. He discovered the nature of plants and metals, including their power in curing diseases and arresting death. But nature had no power to destroy death itself. In all the created things within his reach, he sought the light that would reveal the certainty of eternal life. But he did not find it anywhere. The Book of Truth lay open before him. But its pages were like blank paper. In the Bible, Christianity placed before him the promise of eternal life. But he wanted to read it in his book, where nothing on that subject seemed to have been written.

He had five children—four sons educated as the children of such a wise father should be, and a daughter, who was fair, gentle, and intelligent but also blind. Yet her blindness seemed nothing to her. Her father and brothers were like eyes to her, and a vivid imagination made everything clear in her mind. The sons had never gone farther from the castle than the branches of the trees reached. The sister hardly ever left their home. They were happy children in that home of their childhood, the beautiful and fragrant Tree of the Sun.

Like all children, they loved to hear stories. Their wise father told them many things that other children would not have understood. As a result, these children were as clever as most grown-ups are among us. He explained to them what they saw in the pictures of life on the castle walls—the doings of man and the events in all the lands on the earth. The sons often expressed a wish that they could be present and take part in these great deeds. Then their father told them that in the world there was nothing but toil and difficulty, that things were not as they seemed when viewed from their beautiful home.

He spoke to them of the true, the beautiful and the good. He told them that these three held together the world. He told them that their union was a precious jewel, clearer than the best of diamonds, a jewel whose splendor had value even to God, and in whose brightness all other things seemed dim. This jewel was called the Jewel of Wisdom. He told them that by searching man could attain to a knowledge of the existence of God, and that it was in the power of every man to discover with certainty that the Jewel of Wisdom really existed. This information would have been beyond other children. But these children understood. In time, others will come to understand its meaning too.

They questioned their father about the true, the beautiful, and the good. He explained it to them in many ways. He told them that God, when He made man out of the dust of the earth, touched His work five times, leaving five intense feelings, which we call the five senses. Through these, the true, the beautiful, and the good are seen and understood. Through these, they are also valued, protected and encouraged. Five senses have been given mentally and bodily, inwardly and outwardly, to our bodies and souls.

Day and night, the children thought deeply about these things. Then the eldest of the brothers had an amazing dream. Strange to say, not only the second brother but also the third and fourth brothers all dreamed exactly the same dream. In it, each went out into the world to find the Jewel of Wisdom. Each imagined that he had found it and was riding back to his father's home in the morning dawn on a swift horse over green meadows. As he did so, the stone gleamed from his forehead like a beaming light and threw such a bright radiance on the pages of the Book of Truth that every word was illuminated which spoke of the life beyond the grave. But the sister had no dream of going out into the wide world. It never entered her mind. Her world was her father's house.

The First Brother, the Seer

"I will ride out into the wide world," said the eldest brother. "I must test what life is like there by mixing with men. I will practice only the good and true. With these I will protect the beautiful. Many things will be changed for the better because I am there."

Now these thoughts were great and daring. That is how our thoughts often are at home before we go out into the world and face its storms and tempests as well as its thorns and thistles. In him, as in all his brothers, the five senses were highly developed. But each brother had one sense whose keenness was greater than the other four.

In the case of the eldest, his most powerful sense was sight, which he hoped would be of special service. As the Seer, he had eyes for all times and all people, eyes that could discover in the depths of the earth hidden treasures and look into the hearts of men as through a pane of glass. He could read more than most from the cheek that blushes or grows pale and the eye that droops or smiles.

Deer and antelope accompanied the first brother to the western boundary of his home. There he found wild swans, which he followed until he found himself far away in the north, far from the land of his father, which extended eastward to the ends of the earth.

How his eyes were opened in amazement! How many things were to be seen here, things so different from the pictures he had seen at home. At first he nearly lost his eyes in disgust at the trash and mockery that some claimed represented the beautiful. But he kept his eyes and soon found much for them to do. He wished to work, thoroughly and honestly, to understand the true, the beautiful, and the good. But how are they seen in this world? He saw that the honor which should go to the beautiful was often given the ugly. He saw that the good was often passed by unnoticed. He found that mediocrity was applauded, when it should have been hissed. Sadly, people often looked at the clothes rather than the wearer. They thought more of fame than of doing what was right. They trusted in appearances more than those who had done real service. Everywhere it was the same.

"I must attack this folly," he said, and in this he spared no one. But while looking so hard for the truth, the evil one, the father of lies, entrapped him. Gladly would the fiend have plucked out the eyes of this Seer, but that would have been too straightforward. Instead, he worked more cunningly. He allowed the young man to seek for and discover the beautiful and the good. But while he was contemplating them, the evil spirit blew one tiny speck after another into the oldest son's eyes. These specks were made of something that would injure even the strongest sight. Then he blew on the specks, and they became like a large beam of wood, so the clearness of the young man's sight was lost. As a result, the Seer became like a blind man, and he lost all faith in the world. He lost his good opinion of people, as well as of himself. When a man gives up the world and himself, it is all over with him.

"All over," said the wild swan, who flew across the sea to the east.

"All over," twittered the swallows, who were also flying eastward towards the Tree of the Sun. The news they carried home was bad.

The Second Brother, the Hearer

"I think the Seer has done badly," said the second brother, "but the Hearer may prove more successful."

This brother had very sensitive hearing. So powerful was this sense, that some said he could hear the grass grow. As the Hearer, he said a fond farewell to everyone at home and rode away, filled with good abilities and good intentions. The swallows went with him, and he followed the swans, until he too found himself far from home.

He soon discovered that one can have too much of a good thing. His hearing was too sensitive. He not only heard the grass grow, but he could hear every man's heart beat, whether in sorrow or joy. The whole world was like a giant clock maker's workshop. All the small clocks were going "tick, tick," while all the large clocks struck out the hour with a loud "dong, dong." It was more than he could bear. For a long time his ears endured it, but at last all the noise and tumult became too much for one man to bear.

There were evil boys of sixty years old—for years alone do not make a man—who raised a fuss. That might have simply made the Hearer laugh, but for the applause which followed them, echoing through every street, house and country road. Lies thrust themselves forward and acted like hypocrites. The bells on the fool's cap jingled and claimed to be church bells. For the hearer, the noise became so unbearable that he thrust his fingers into his ears. That did little good. He could still hear false notes and bad singing, gossip and idle words, scandal and slander, groaning and moaning, without and within.

He thrust his fingers farther and farther into his ears, until at last his eardrums burst. Now he could hear nothing of the true, the beautiful, and the good. He became silent and suspicious. He trusted no one, not even himself. No longer hoping to bring home the costly jewel, he gave up on his dream. He gave up on himself too, which was the worst of all.

The birds in their flight towards the east carried the tidings, and the news reached the castle in the Tree of the Sun.

The Third Brother, the Poet

"I will try now," said the third brother. "I have a keen nose." Now that was not a very elegant thing to say. But it was his way of talking, and we must take him as he was. He had a cheerful temper and was a talented poet. He could make many ideas seem like poetry just by the way he described them.

Ideas struck him long before they came to others. He believed that the sense of smelling, which he had in a high degree, gave him a great power to sense beauty. "I can smell," he would say, "and many places are fragrant or beautiful according to the taste of those who come there. One man feels at home in a tavern among the cheap candles, where the smell of alcohol mingles with the fumes of bad tobacco. Another would rather sit surrounded by the overpowering scent of jasmine or chooses to perfume himself with scented olive oil. One seeks the fresh sea breeze, while another climbs a lofty mountain top to look down on the busy life in miniature beneath him."

As he spoke like that, it seemed as if he had already been out in the world. It seemed as if he had already known and associated with man. But this experience was intuitive—it was the poetry within him, a gift that Heaven had given him in the cradle. As the Poet, he said farewell to his parents in the Tree of the Sun and left behind the pleasant scenes of his home. Arriving at the border of the land, he mounted on the back of an ostrich, which runs faster than a horse. When he met wild swans, he swung himself on the strongest of them, for he loved change and speed.

Away he flew over the sea to distant lands, where there were great forests, deep lakes, lofty mountains, and proud cities. Wherever he went, sunshine traveled across the fields with him. Every flower and bush released a fragrance, knowing that a friend and protector was near, one who understood them and knew their value. The stunted rosebush shot out twigs, unfolded its leaves, and bore the most beautiful roses. Everyone could see it. Even the black, slimy wood snail noticed its beauty. "I give my seal to the flower," said the snail. "I have trailed my slime on it, I can do no more."

"This is how it always goes with the beautiful in this world," said the Poet. He made a song about what he had seen and sung it in his own style. But nobody listened. Then he gave a drummer two pennies and a peacock's feather, and composed a song for the drum. The drummer beat it through the streets of the town. When the people heard it, they said, "That is a delightful tune." The poet wrote many songs about the true, the beautiful, and the good. His songs were listened to in the tavern, where the tallow candles flared, in the fresh clover field, in the forest, and on the high seas.

It looked like this brother would be more fortunate than the previous two. But the evil spirit was angry at this. So he set to work with soot and incense, which he could mix artfully enough to confuse an angel, how much more the poor Poet. The evil one knew how to manage such people. He surrounded the Poet with so much incense, that the man lost his head, forgetting his dream and his home. At last, he lost himself and vanished into the smoke.

But when the little birds heard of it, they mourned. For three days they sang not one song. The black wood snail became blacker still, not from grief, but from envy. "They should have offered me incense," he said, "for it was I who gave him the idea of the most famous of his songs—the drum song of 'The Way of the World.' It was I who spat at the rose. I can bring a witness to that fact."

But no news of this reached the Poet's home in India. The birds had all been silent for three days. When the time of mourning was over, so deep had been their grief, that they forgot for whom they wept. Such is the way of the world.

The Fourth Brother, the Taster

"Now I must go out into the world and disappear like the rest," said the fourth brother. He was as good-tempered as the third, but he was no poet, although he could be witty.

The eldest two brothers had filled the castle with joy. Now the last brightness was fading away. Sight and hearing have always been considered the two chief senses among men and those we value the most. The other senses are looked on as less important.

But the younger son had a different opinion. He had cultivated his taste in every way, and taste is very powerful. It rules over what goes into the mouth, as well as over all that is presented to the mind. As a result, this brother took it on himself to taste everything stored up in bottles or jars. As the Taster, he called this the rough part of his work. Every man's mind was to him as a vessel in which something was being cooked. Every land was a kitchen of the mind. "There are no delicacies here," he said. Now he wanted to go into the world to find something delicious enough to suit his taste. "Perhaps fortune will be more favorable to me than to my brothers. I will start on my travels, but what means of travel will I choose? Are balloons invented yet?" he asked of his father, who knew of all inventions that had been made or would be made. Balloons had not been invented, nor steamships, nor railways.

"Good," said he. "then I will choose a balloon. My father knows how they are made and guided. Nobody has invented one yet, so the people will believe that it is a flying spirit. When I have done with the balloon, I will burn it. For this purpose you must give me another invention that is still to come, a few matches."

He got what he wanted from his father and flew away. The birds accompanied him farther than they had the other brothers. They were curious to know how his flight would end. Many came swooping down on the brother and his balloon. They thought this must be some new bird, and so he soon had a large company of flying followers. They came in clouds until the sky was as darkened with birds as it was when the cloud of locusts came over the land of Egypt in Moses's day.

Now he was out in the world. His balloon came down on one of the largest cities in the world and at the highest point in that city, the top of the church steeple. The balloon rose again into the air, which it ought not to have done. What became of it no one knows. It doesn't matter. Balloons had not yet been invented.

There he sat on the top of church steeple. The birds no longer flew around him. They had grown tired of him, and he of them.

All the chimneys in the town were smoking. "They are altars erected in my honor," said the wind, who wished to say something agreeable to the brother as he sat boldly looking down on the people in the street. There was one stepping along, proud of his wealth. Another was proud of the key he carried with him, even though he had nothing to lock up. Yet another took pride in his moth-eaten coat, and another, in his deliberately starved body.

"Vanity, all is vanity!" the fourth son cried out. "I must go down there by-and-by to touch and to taste. But I will sit here a little longer, for the wind blows pleasantly at my back. I shall stay here and enjoy a little rest as long as the wind blows the same direction. It is comfortable to sleep late in the morning when one has much to do," said the lazy brother. "So I shall rest here, for it pleases me."

There he stayed. But, as he was sitting on the weather cock of the steeple, which kept turning around and around with him, he was under the mistaken impression that the same wind still blew. He also believed that he could stay where he was without paying a price.

But in India, in the castle on the Tree of the Sun, all was sad and lonely since the brothers had gone away, one after the other.

"Nothing goes well with them," said the father. "They will never bring the glittering jewel home. It is not made for me. They are all dead and gone." Then he bent down over the Book of Truth and gazed on the page on which he should have read of the life after death. But for him there was nothing to read or learn on it.

The Daughter, the Believer

His blind daughter became the father's only consolation and joy. She clung to him with a great love. For the sake of his happiness and peace, she wished the costly jewel could be found and brought home.

With much tenderness she thought of her brothers. Where were they? Where did they live? She wanted to dream some news about them. But not even in her dreams was she be brought near to them.

At last one night she dreamed that she heard the voices of her brothers calling out to her from the distant world. She could not restrain herself, and in her dream she went out to them. Yet it seemed in her dream that she still remained in her father's house. She did not see her brothers, but she felt as if the thought of them was a fire burning in her hand, a fire that did not hurt her. For the thought of them was the jewel that she was bringing to her father. When she awoke, she thought for a moment that she still held the stone. But she found that all she held in her hand was the knob of her spinning staff.

During the long evenings she spun constantly. Around her spinning staff were threads finer than the web of a spider. Human eyes could never have seen these threads when they were separated from each other. But she wetted them with her tears, and though they were thin, they were as strong as steel cable. She began to believe that her dream must be real, and thus her mind was made up.

It was still night and her father slept. She pressed a kiss on his hand. Then she took her spinning staff and fastened one end of the thread to her father's house. But for this, blind as she was, she would never find her way home again. To this thread she must hold tightly, and trust not to others or to herself. From the Tree of the Sun she broke four leaves, which she gave to the wind and the weather, that they might be carried to her brothers as letters and a greeting, in case she did not meet them in the wide world.

Poor blind child, what would happen to her in distant lands? But she had the invisible thread, which she could hold fast. She also had a gift that the others lacked—the determination to throw herself completely into her mission. It made her feel as if she had eyes on the tips of her fingers and could hear into her own heart.

Quietly she went into the noisy, bustling, wonderful world. Wherever she went, the skies grew bright. She felt the warm sunbeam. A rainbow in the blue heavens above seemed to span across the dark world. She heard the song of the birds and smelled the scent of the orange groves and apple orchards so strongly that she seemed to taste them. Soft tones and charming songs reached her ear, as well as harsh sounds and rough words. Thoughts and opinions in strange contradiction to each other came to her mind. The deepest recesses of her heart penetrated into the echoes of human thoughts and feelings. Then she heard the following words sadly sung:

> Life is a shadow that flits away
> In a night of darkness and woe.

But then would follow brighter thoughts:

> Life has the rose's sweet perfume
> With sunshine, light and joy.

And if one stanza sounded painful:

> Each mortal thinks of himself alone,
> Is a truth, alas, too clearly known.

Then, on the other hand, came the answer:

> Love, like a mighty flowing stream,
> Fills every heart with its radiant gleam.

She heard, indeed, such words as these:

In the pretty turmoil here below,

All is a vain and paltry show.

Then came also words of comfort:

Great and good are the actions done

By many whose worth is never known.

And if sometimes the mocking strain reached her:

Why not join in the jesting cry

That condemns all gifts from the throne on high?

In the blind girl's heart a stronger voice repeated:

To trust in thyself and God is best,

In His holy will forever to rest.

Of course, the evil spirit could not see this happen and remain content. He has more cleverness than ten thousand men, and he always found a way to carry out his plans. He went to a marsh and collected a few bubbles of stagnant water. Then he uttered over them the echoes of lying words that they might become strong. He mixed together songs of praise with lying oaths, as many as he could find. He boiled them in tears shed by envy, put on them red rouge, which he had scraped from faded cheeks. From these he produced a maiden, looking very much like the blind girl, the angel of completeness, as men called her. The evil one's plot was successful. The world knew not which was the true, and indeed how should it know?

To trust in thyself and God is best,

In his Holy will forever to rest.

So sung the blind girl in full faith. She had entrusted the four green leaves from the Tree of the Sun to the winds as letters of greeting to her brothers. She had full confidence that the leaves would reach them. She believed that the jewel which outshines all the glories of the world would still be found. She believed that on the forehead of humanity it would glitter in the castle of her father.

"Even in my father's house," she repeated. "Yes, the place where this jewel is to be found is earth. I will bring more than the promise of it with me. I feel it glow more and more in my closed hand. Every grain of truth that the keen wind carried up and whirled around me, I caught and treasured. I allowed it to be penetrated with the fragrance of the beautiful, of which there is so much in the world even for the blind. I took the beatings of a heart engaged in a good deed and added them to my treasure. All that I can bring is but dust. Still, it is a part of the jewel we seek. There is plenty, my hand is quite full of it."

She soon found herself again at home. She was carried there in a flight of thought, never having loosened her hold of the invisible thread that was fastened to her father's house. As she stretched out her hand to her father, the powers of evil dashed with the fury of a hurricane over the Tree of the Sun. A blast of wind rushed through the open doors and into the sanctuary, where the Book of Truth lay.

"It will be blown to pieces by the wind," said the father, as he seized the open hand she held out to him.

"No," she replied, with quiet confidence, "it is indestructible. I feel its beam warming my very soul."

Then her father saw that a dazzling flame gleamed from the white page on which the shining dust had passed from her hand. What was written there proved the certainty of eternal life. On that page in the book, the book glowed one shining word and only one, the word was "Believe." Soon the four brothers were again with their father and sister. When the green leaf from home had fallen on the chest of each, a longing to return home had seized them. They had arrived, accompanied by migrating birds, the deer, the antelope, and all the creatures of the forest who wished to join in their joy.

We have often seen, when a sunbeam burst through a crack in the door into a dusty room, how a whirling column of dust seems to circle around. But this was not poor, insignificant, common dust that the blind girl had brought. Even the rainbow's colors are dim when compared with the beauty that shone from the page on which it had fallen. The word "Believe" beaming from every grain of truth, had the brightness of the beautiful and the good, more bright than the mighty pillar of flame that led Moses and the children of Israel to the land of Canaan. From the word "Believe" arose the bridge of hope, reaching even to the unmeasurable Love in the realms of the infinite.

—§§§—

14. The Snowdrop

*A brave flower reminds everyone of the promise of spring and
of a poet whose public life mirrored that of the flower.
Reading time: 15 minutes. All ages.*

It was winter. Outside, the air was cold and the wind was sharp and biting, but inside the little house it was warm and comfortable. Just outside its door a little flower called a Snowdrop lay sleeping within a flower bulb that was buried deep in the snow-covered ground.

One day rain fell instead of snow. The rain drops soaked through the snow and into the ground. They touched the Snowdrop's bulb, awoke her and told her of the world above. Then a Sunbeam, filled with warmth and light, pierced through the snow to the root of that little Snowdrop. There was a stirring as the flower woke up.

"Come in," said the Snowdrop.

"I cannot," said the Sunbeam. "I am not strong enough to unlock the door! But when summer comes, I *will* be strong enough!"

"When will it be summer?" asked the Snowdrop longingly. She repeated this question every time a new Sunbeam made its way down to her. But summer was still far away. The snow lay on the ground, and a coat of ice covered the pond every night.

"What a long time it takes for summer to come!" said the Snowdrop, sadly. "I feel something stirring inside me. I must stretch myself and get out of bed. I want to unlock the door and go out into the world. I want to wave good morning to the summer. What a happy time that will be!"

Then the Snowdrop stirred and stretched within her bulb. The water from the rain had softened her shell. The Sunshine had knocked on her door and warmed the earth around her. The Snowdrop shot up from under the snow with a greenish-white blossom on a green stalk and with narrow thick leaves that protected her from the cold like a blanket. The snow was very cold, but it was pierced by the warming Sunbeam, so it was soft and easy to get through. Now that the Snowdrop was on the surface of the ground, the Sunbeam could visit her with warmth and light even better than before.

"Welcome, welcome!" sang every Sunbeam. The Snowdrop lifted itself out of the snow and into the bright world. The Sunbeams caressed and kissed it, so that it opened up its petals, white as snow and marked with green stripes. It bent its head in joy and humility.

"Beautiful Snowdrop!" said the Sunbeams. "How graceful and delicate you are! You are the first to bloom! You are the only one who is blooming now! You are our one true love! You are the bell that rings out for summer, beautiful summer, over country and town. You promise us that the snow will melt and the cold winds be driven away. As Sunbeams, we will rule over nature and everything will be green and beautiful again. Then you will have other flowers to keep you company, syringas, laburnums, and roses. But you are the very first, so graceful and so delicate!"

Those words made the Snowdrop very happy. She felt like the air was singing and leaping about. She felt as if rays of light were falling on her leaves and stalks, warming them. There she stood, so delicate and easily broken and yet so strong in her young beauty. She stood there in her white dress with green stripes and told everyone of the summer-to-be.

But then something sad happened. Summer, it seemed, was still a long time away. Clouds hid the sun, and bleak, cold winds blew.

STORIES FOR GIRLS

"You have come too early," said the Wind and Weather, taunting her. "Sunbeams do not rule. We still have the power. You will soon feel it and give proper respect to us. You should have stayed quietly in your home under the ground and not come out to make a silly show of yourself. Your time is not yet here!"

The cold cut like a knife! The days that followed brought not a single Sunbeam. The cold seemed powerful enough to cut the little Snowdrop in two. But the Snowdrop had more strength than she herself knew. She was strong in joy and trusted in the summer which was sure to come. Her deep longing promised that summer would come. So she remained standing bravely in the snow in her white garment, bending her head, even while the snowflakes fell thick and heavy, and the icy winds swept over her.

"You'll break!" said the Wind and Weather, "and fade and fade! What do you want out here? Why did you let yourself be tempted into coming out? The Sunbeam only made game of you. Now you have what you deserve, you Summer Fool."

"Summer Fool!" the Snowdrop said to herself in the cold morning hour. Summer Fool was another name for the Snowdrop.

"O Summer Fool!" cried some children rejoicingly. "There is one—how beautiful she is, how beautiful! The first one, the only one!"

These happy words by children did the Snowdrop much good. They were like warm Sunbeams. In her joy the Snowdrop did not even notice when it was broken off. She lay in a child's hand, was kissed by a child's mouth, and carried into a warm room. She was looked at by gentle, admiring eyes and put in water. How wonderful the warm room seemed! The Snowdrop thought summer had come in an instant.

Now it happened that the daughter of the house, a beautiful girl, was confirmed at church. She had a friend who was confirmed, too. He was studying for an examination, so he could be appointed to a job.

"He will be my Summer Fool," she said teasingly. Then she took the delicate Snowdrop and laid her in a piece of scented paper on which some verses of poetry were written, beginning with "Summer Fool" and ending with "Summer Fool." "My friend, be a Winter Fool." She teased him about the summer.

Yes, all this was in the verses. The paper was folded up like a letter, and the Snowdrop was folded inside the letter. It was now dark around that Snowdrop, as dark as in the days when she lay hidden in the bulb underneath the ground. The Snowdrop went on her journey. She lay in the postman's bag for days and was pressed and crushed in the mail, which was not at all pleasant. But that soon came to an end.

The journey was over. The letter was opened and read by the dear friend. How pleased he was! He kissed the letter. It was laid, with the verses the girl had written, in a box in which there were many beautiful verses, but all the rest were without flowers. Our little Snowdrop was the first one and the only one, just as the Sunbeam had said. That was a happy thing to think about.

The Snowdrop had time enough and more to think. She thought while the summer passed away and the long winter came and went. The summer came again before she appeared before the young man once more. But now he was not happy at all. He took hold of the letter very roughly and threw the verses away. The poor Snowdrop fell on the floor. Flat and faded she certainly was, but why should she be thrown away? Still, it was better to be here than in the fire, where the verses and the paper were now being burnt to ashes. What had happened? What happens so often—the Snowdrop had made a fool of the young man in jest. The girl had made a fool of him and that was no jest. She had, during the summer, chosen another boy friend.

The next morning the sun shone on the little flattened Snowdrop, who looked as if she had been painted on the floor. The servant girl, who was sweeping out the room, picked her up, and laid her in one of the books on the table, believing she must have fallen out while the room was being arranged. Again the flower lay among verses, printed verses this time. They are better than written ones, or at least, more money had been spent on them.

Years went by. The book stood unused on the bookshelf, and then somebody took it down to read from it. It was a good book, with verses and songs by the old Danish poet, Ambrosius Stub, which are well worth reading. The man who was now reading the book turned over a page.

"Why, there's a flower!" he said. "A Snowdrop, a Summer Fool, a Poet Fool! That flower must have been put in there with a meaning! Poor Ambrosius Stub! He was a Summer Fool too and a Poet Fool. He came too early, before his time, and so he had to taste the sharp winds of rejection and wander about as a guest from one wealthy supporter's home to another, like a flower in a glass of water, a flower in rhymed verses! Summer Fool, Winter Fool, fun and folly. But he was the first, the only, the fresh young Danish poet of those days. Yes, you will remain as a special reminder in the book, you little Snowdrop. You have been put there with a meaning."

So the Snowdrop was put back into the book. She felt equally honored and pleased to know that she was a special reminder in a glorious book of songs. He who was the first to sing and to write had also been a Snowdrop, a Summer Fool. He had also been looked on in the winter as a fool. The Snowdrop understood this, in her own way, much as we see everything in our way.

That, my friend, is the story of the Snowdrop.

Printed in the United Kingdom
by Lightning Source UK Ltd.
124664UK00001B/115/A